MW01612854

C 2016 by Jon Horner

The Flight of the Slacker

By

Jon Horner

To Darla, Chase, Madison, my parents, Bill and Adella Horner; Don and Linda Blades, Danny and Kay Sims, and to the numerous people who have asked for my next novel and reached out to offer encouragement to continue writing.

MILFORD T Blanchard, Jr., otherwise known as Gordy by his family and friends in the quaint town of Bouvier, located in the beautiful Ozark hills of Barry County, Missouri; was heading to work on a sunny day in September. It seemed like any other day, but today would be a day that would change the life of Gordy Blanchard and eventually impact the entire community of Bouvier, in a way that no other event had ever touched the town.

Growing up as the son of a highly respected community leader had placed tremendous pressure to succeed upon Gordy Blanchard. This type of pressure would be difficult for most mortals, but it was especially burdensome for a slacker like Gordy. His father was Milford T. Blanchard, who served for decades as Superintendent of the Bouvier School System. His reign was so acclaimed that upon his retirement, the Bouvier Board of Education named the school administration building in his honor and funded an annual scholarship for the graduating Valedictorian in his name.

As Gordy was driving to work, there were no visions of a future Gordy Blanchard Academic Center for Excellence on the horizon at the Bouvier School District. No, as Gordy was pulling into his parking spot at the Milford T. Blanchard Administration Building, Gordy felt lucky to simply be employed at all. And he knew deep down, that if it weren't for his father's legacy in Bouvier, he would more than likely be coaching golf and teaching history, which is what he really wanted to be doing with his life.

Gordy Blanchard was a very intelligent young man. He was six foot and two inches tall, with a full head of black hair. By any standards, he was very handsome, personable, and looked the part of a budding young professional. But the drive and ambition that had made his father a near legend in the education field had totally escaped Gordy Blanchard. His friends whispered that Gordy was a lovable slacker, who would have been content to live a simple life as a coach and teacher, in a small farmhouse or a river cabin. But that life had never been an option for Gordy. His parents had selected his career path before he had left eighth grade and then the turbo charged ambition of his social climbing wife, Elizabeth, sealed his fate. Now, his position as Assistant Superintendent of the Bouvier School System had placed him at both a pinnacle of success and as a miserable failure.

As Gordy Blanchard departed his blue Ford 150 four-wheel drive truck, he was about to set in motion a series of events never seen before in Bouvier. But the question that kept going through Gordy's mind was, "How did I get myself into this situation and was there any other alternative to what he had decided to do?" Unfortunately, Gordy's desperate state of mind had robbed him of the ability to process rational alternatives to his plight. As the old saying goes, desperate people do desperate things. That phrase described Gordy Blanchard to a tee on this September morning in Bouvier. The sad irony of the moment was that the slacker had become quite ingenious as his personal and professional life began to spiral out of control.

Planning had never been one of Gordy's strengths. Now when placed in a terribly embarrassing and comprising situation Gordy realized that he would have to set up an elaborate plan to escape the mess that he had helped create. He had reluctantly realized months earlier that there wasn't any way he could face what would happen when his mistakes became known. As he reflected on his actions that had placed him in this desperate position, he was sickened by the fact that his inability to use good judgment and self-control had led to his downfall. Now ironically, desperate planning and focus on his goal of flight were the very things guiding his plan to escape his embarrassing plight. He kept wondering if his plan was rational and could he possibly escape this terrible situation without doing what he was about to set in motion. As he looked around the offices of the Milford T. Blanchard administration offices, Gordy concluded that he had no choice but to go through with his plan. He was deeply saddened because for his plan to work there would be no opportunity to tell those close to him how sorry he was for his shortcomings.

Before he made the final act to escape his desperate situation, Gordy walked around his office and took in the sights, smells, and unique features that had been a part of most of his adult life. When he was growing up in Bouvier, Gordy's office had been the men's locker room for his Junior High basketball team. The thoughts of his happy childhood, playing ball in Bouvier, and getting ready for practice each day came rushing back. They made him wonder more and more why and how he was now in a place he saw as a point of no return.

Gordy ached for the innocent days when the worst thing that could happen to you was losing to one of Bouvier's archrivals, Mt. Vernon, Aurora, or Seneca. As he looked around the walls of his office for the final time, Gordy's mind was set. He had to go through with his plan. Unfortunately, he saw no other choice. Gordy just couldn't face his family, life-long friends, co-workers, and his former students with his sins and moral weaknesses.

As he was getting ready to exit his office, Gordy looked fondly at his golf trophy for winning the Big 8 championship as a senior at Bouvier High. This was right next to the Big 8 championship trophy that Bouvier won the first year Gordy was their golf coach. Those two events had been the most enjoyable moments of Gordy's personal and professional life in Bouvier. Before he walked out, Gordy placed his high school class ring in a strategic place; one that would prove to be important in the days to follow. For Gordy it was a sentimental goodbye to a time in his life that at one time had held so much promise. As he made his exit, Gordy wiped away a tear as he said, "Good bye, Bouvier."

Chapter 2

The question of "why was a slacker like Gordy working early on a Sunday morning," puzzled his father, Milford T. Blanchard. It also drew the attention of Gordy's boss, Bouvier Superintendent of Schools, Baxter Flynn. Flynn had started his coaching career with Gordy and they were very close friends. Baxter Flynn knew Gordy Blanchard's failings better than anyone else, probably more so than his family. Flynn was in his mid 30s and had become the Superintendent of the Bouvier School System during the prior academic year. Possessing the ambition and the desire to move up the administrative ladder that had escaped his good friend, Flynn became Superintendent much sooner than he had anticipated, as his predecessor had abruptly departed for a similar position in a rival community. This was not long before it was discovered that Flynn's predecessor had become a little too cozy and supportive of a pregnant high school cheerleading coach.

Flynn was the person who recruited Gordy as his number two guy. Having been thrust into the Superintendent position much faster than he had wanted, Flynn felt as if he needed and could trust Gordy as he navigated the politically charged waters of the Bouvier community. Plus, by having him on board also meant he had the support of the legendary Milford T. Blanchard.

Flynn had realized Gordy had been "preoccupied" during the past few weeks. He automatically assumed that things weren't going well between Gordy and his wife, Elizabeth. Gordy had been working more hours than ever before, even working a few Sunday mornings.

Elizabeth Blanchard had never been happy with her and Gordy's plight in life, but it seemed that she had been more and more demanding of Gordy during the last year. The ambition that Gordy lacked was compensated by his wife's turbo charged ambition and zest to move up the professional and social ladder.

Elizabeth was a third grade teacher in the Bouvier School System and was a striking beauty. Standing five foot eleven with flowing auburn hair, Elizabeth easily commanded any man's attention, especially Gordy's.

Ever the gossip hound, she had heard the rumors that Gordy's job performance as Assistant Superintendent had been less than stellar. The Auditor's report from the prior year was a damning indictment of Gordy's accounting practices, or lack thereof, and unfortunately the report was a public document available for anyone to see, including Elizabeth Blanchard. She took the criticism as a personal affront on her standing in the community.

Ever the social climber, Elizabeth continually ridiculed Gordy for embarrassing the family due to his shortcomings as an administrator. The common refrain was, "How could you be so incompetent? Your father would never have had an audit go like this. You need to pull your head out of your ass and stop embarrassing us and your family........" Clearly there wasn't any nurturing for Gordy's fractured confidence and self esteem from Elizabeth and this only added to the mounting pressure on him as he approached another year's audit of the school's books.

Flynn knew the upcoming audit was of great concern to Gordy. As Gordy's close friend and his boss, he was greatly aware of the level of embarrassment Gordy had suffered when the critical audit had been released the prior year. He encouraged Gordy to receive training to strengthen his accounting managerial skills, but Flynn sensed that things were not as they should be despite Gordy's contention that he had his deficiencies corrected and things would be much better this time around for the school audit. Flynn believed that Gordy's shortcomings had more to do with his inability to assert his authority within his office than his attention to detail. He worried that Gordy was either being manipulated or outright lied to by one of his staff members. Flynn didn't have any ironclad proof of it, so he continually delayed confronting Gordy with his gut feeling. He was going to let the upcoming audit confirm or dissuade his sense of what might be going on. The audit would either confirm Gordy's assertions that he had corrected the vast deficiencies, or worst case, put Baxter Flynn in the horrible position of having to fire his best friend. So Flynn was as worried as anyone else about the approaching audit.

Now as he paced the parking lot and faced the fire raging out of what had once been the Milford T. Blanchard Administrative Building, Baxter Flynn was barely able to contain his emotions. Seeing Gordy's pickup truck situated next to the Bouvier fire trucks made him sick. Baxter desperately hoped that Gordy's death was instantaneous and painless. Losing your best friend in an inexplicable explosion is one thing, but having to immediately move forward and put together a temporary administration office made it worse. Baxter Flynn wasn't sure if he could pull it off. He wanted to just go off into the woods and hide for a few days to allow himself time to come to grips with what had happened. But with the 3,000 school kids, their parents, and the Bouvier community looking to him for leadership in this horrible time, Flynn would have to muster the courage to move forward and find a way mourn for his best friend. The question of "why was he here on a Sunday morning?" would have to be answered another time and day, if ever.

The explosion rocked Bouvier in a way that long-time locals had never seen or heard during their lifetimes. The time would be etched in the memories of those in Bouvier for many reasons. First, the death of Gordy Blanchard shook the town just as the physical nature of the explosion that took his young life. Second, the legendary clock tower at the center of the Bouvier school campus was permanently frozen at the time of 5:56 am, which was the precise time of the explosion in the Milford T. Blanchard administration building. Many questions were being asked about the horrible events on that beautiful September morning, but more than likely, most would remain unanswered.

The phone call to Milford T. Blanchard was the hardest thing Baxter Flynn had ever had to do in his life. Telling someone that they have lost a loved one is never easy, but having to tell someone whom you respect like a father made it worse.

Blanchard had heard the sirens and then had picked up from Facebook that there was an explosion at the school. Upon hearing the news of an explosion at the school, Nancy Blanchard, Gordy's mother, immediately told Milford that she feared something was wrong with Gordy.

Call it mother's intuition or an inner gut instinct; Nancy was worried about her son. She called Gordy's cell phone three times to no avail. She then called Elizabeth's cell phone. The first call went unanswered, but Nancy tried again. This time she woke up a very irritated Elizabeth Blanchard. Elizabeth hadn't heard the sirens and didn't know Gordy wasn't home.

When Nancy asked to talk to Gordy, Elizabeth couldn't find him or his pickup truck. It was then Elizabeth had awakened enough to remember Gordy mentioning the night before that he might go down to the school and get some things done before church and his usual Sunday round of golf with his buddies. Upon hearing this, Nancy Blanchard feared the worst.

The phone call from Baxter Flynn confirmed her mother's intuition. Baxter informed the Blanchard's that it didn't look good. Gordy's truck was the only truck in the parking lot when the fire department arrived. It would be days before the fire would be cooled down enough to search for a body.

The decision was made by Flynn and Blanchard that it would be best if they went together to deliver the news to Elizabeth. Flynn had never been a big fan of Elizabeth, so having Milford Blanchard with him was a great relief. He knew how cruel Elizabeth could be and he worried that he might lose his cool if she were to let loose on one of her patented childish tantrums. Flynn sensed she would be on her best behavior in the presence of her beloved father-in-law.

Flynn arrived at the Gordy and Elizabeth Blanchard residence a couple of minutes before Milford Blanchard. As he waited, Flynn took in the sights of the Blanchard home. The brick front was beautiful and the flowers adorning the front walkway were picturesque. Clearly, Elizabeth Blanchard took great pride in the appearance of their home. Flynn thought that was very fitting, as Elizabeth was all about appearances. Gordy Blanchard was as down to earth a person that Baster Flynn had ever met. He wondered today, as he had many times before, how did Gordy ever get hooked up with someone like Elizabeth. He feared he would never get the opportunity to broach that question with his dear friend.

When Flynn and Blanchard arrived at the front door Elizabeth was in tears. The call from Nancy Blanchard had aroused her fears. She immediately had gone to Facebook to see the numerous posts about an explosion at the Blanchard Administration Building. The first thing she said when she saw Flynn and her father-in-law was, "He's gone, isn't he? That's why you're here, isn't it?"

Milford Blanchard wrapped his arms around Elizabeth and whispered, "Hon, it doesn't look good for our boy."

Elizabeth was crying uncontrollably and couldn't say anything at the moment other than, "What happened, what happened, how could this happen...?"

Milford wasn't sure what to say at the moment. It was one of the few times in his life that he felt totally helpless. He desperately wanted to be positive, but the reality of the scene at the school was grim. He sat down with Elizabeth and attempted to calm her down.

"Hon, there has been an explosion in the administration building. And Gord's truck is in the parking lot. Had he said anything about working this morning?"

Between sobs, Elizabeth said that the last thing she remembered before going to sleep was Gordy saying he might go get some things done at school before heading to church.

"He didn't wake me before he left. I was still asleep when Nanc called. Have they checked to see if he's walking around the campus or something like that? Is his office the area that's on fire? I just can't believe he's gone. I can't believe it. It can't be." At this point Elizabeth began to sob again uncontrollably.

Flynn stepped forward to answer Elizabeth. He stated that they had walked the campus and had not been able to see Gordy. Before he could finish his sentence, he was abruptly interrupted by Elizabeth.

"Have they really tried or did they just tell you that? Lord knows how lazy some of those guys are. Have you actually looked around for Gordy?"

This was the Elizabeth that Flynn had grown to despise, but he kept his cool for Milford's sake. Before he could attempt to speak again, Milford Blanchard decided to put a stop to any unneeded tension in light of the situation. He calmly spoke to Elizabeth.

"Hon, I know you are afraid and scared. We all are at this moment. I hope and pray that Gord was out walking between buildings when the explosion took place, but right now, it doesn't look good. No one has seen Gordy. His office is gone and the entire administration building is on fire. It's going to take days before anyone can search the building."

Elizabeth became enraged. "You've got to be kidding me. Those guys are going to wait days to search for Gordy? I want them in there first thing in the morning. This is ridiculous. I can't believe it. You would think they would actually turn a tap for Gordy Blanchard of all people." As she ranted, her eyes darted all over the place. Her pink and black pajamas were moving in concert with her arms as she ranted about the situation.

Flynn couldn't help but notice her attractive figure from the outline of her stylish PJs. He assumed that Elizabeth would soon be trying to reel in another poor unsuspecting victim for her affection not long after Gordy was properly memorialized.

Seeing that he needed to get things under control, Blanchard gently tried to get Elizabeth calmed down. He assured her that everyone was doing their best. And then Milford did the one thing that finally caught her attention, he became stern.

"Hon, I know you love Gordy. We all do. But lashing out at people isn't going to make things any better. To be honest, all it will do is make you look bad and we all know you don't want that. Don't act this way. You will regret it if you do. But the choice is yours. What can we do for you at this moment?"

Blanchard's caring but stern words must have hit their mark, because Elizabeth immediately calmed down and became reasonable, much to the relief of her visitors. She hugged Blanchard tightly and gave him a gentle peck on his right cheek. She thanked them for coming and said she would like to get showered before going over to the Blanchard's home.

As she walked her visitors to the door, Flynn couldn't help but feel contempt for Elizabeth Blanchard and sadness for his life-long buddy, Gordy Blanchard. Flynn wondered how bad Gordy's life must have been to be married to someone like Elizabeth, combined with the pressure to live up to the ideal of being Milford Blanchard's son in the town of Bouvier, Missouri. It must have been unbearable. This meeting had opened up Flynn's eyes as to why Gordy had seemed out of touch over the past few months. Little did he know exactly how desperate Gordy Blanchard had become during this time period.

Chapter 3

The scene at Ruby's Pancakes and More on Sunday morning was a surreal setting as the locals began to gather for information, not so much for facts, but for the latest scuttlebutt coming from the school explosion. Ruby's was a legendary Bouvier café known as much for its great gossip as its food. The owner, Emerald Patrick, was a spunky soul who relished in the daily banter with the locals and tourists that frequented her café. Patrick was a transformed soul who had been led to a better life by the influence of Bouvier's fabled Reverend Durwood Hardy, but today Emerald was no where to be found. She was having a difficult time coping with the news about Gordy Blanchard, who had been one of her regulars at the café.

The regulars who frequented the large table at the center of Ruby's, otherwise known as the "Board of Directors Table," were spewing forth their various expert opinions as to what had taken place at the school and why an explosion of that magnitude had happened. Most of the regulars who frequented the "Board" table, local cowboys, construction workers, and part-time farmers, had never been big fans of Gordy Blanchard, who was viewed as a slick professional in their jealous eyes. It seemed that today they had the good sense to hide their jaded opinions of Blanchard as they could see that his presumed death was hitting the Bouvier community extremely hard. No one wanted to be seen as an uncaring jerk on a day like this. The overwhelming opinion of the "experts" at Ruby's was the city's sewer main must have leaked a lethal combination of sewer gases thus causing the powerful explosion at the school. Like usual, the regulars were citing the City of Bouvier as the culprit for the disaster. The common expert opinions coming from the Board table were, "I've been telling those city boys that they needed to check on those sewer lines. But they're too damn lazy to go over and see if something's wrong." And "If I were running that sewer department, I would fire half of those lazy bastards."

As the regulars continued to pour in on that fateful morning, one thing clearly caught the attention of the folks at Ruby's; Emerald Patrick wasn't in the café. This didn't go unnoticed by the good ole boys at the Board Table.

As much as they held their tongues with regard for their true feelings for Gordy Blanchard, they couldn't help but offer some perspective on what they had noticed over the past few months in the café. It appeared a glowing friendship was developing between Emerald and Gordy.

Gordy had started frequenting Ruby's on a regular basis over the past six months. He tried to come in early to avoid the Board of Directors crowd, who obviously held him in great distain. Since he came in around the time the café opened, Emerald was always the one who waited on Gordy.

Emerald's spunky streak came to life when Gordy would order breakfast. Gordy would usually order a plain waffle with maple syrup and a regular coffee laden with cream. She quickly sensed that he was down on himself and needed a shot in the arm from a psychological standpoint. Emerald sensed that Gordy was coming in for more than just breakfast as he continued to come in each morning at the same time. He was there to see her and have someone to talk with in a playful banter that was clearly missing from his relationship with his wife Elizabeth. Emerald came to realize the Gordy was quite fond of her wisecracks about his eating habits.

"Let's see Gord, today you're going to have a waffle, or are you going to venture out and possibly try something really adventurous like a plain pancake? Come on Gord, go for it, take the challenge and order a pancake for heaven's sake."

Gordy would smile and order his waffle, but he eventually started to open up to Emerald's cute but intrusive questions about his job, activities, and family life. In addition to an infectious personality, Emerald was a beautiful young lady. Standing five foot seven with long auburn hair, Emerald was hard not to notice. Additionally, she has used some of her hard earned café profits for a striking breast enhancement. As a result, it was easy to see why Gordy was becoming smitten with Emerald.

As the months turned over on the calendar, the time Gordy spent each morning in Ruby's increased to the point that many in the café began to take notice of the coziness between Emerald and Gordy. Despite being completely self-absorbed and having little interest in her husband, other than his professional standing, Elizabeth caught wind of his growing friendship with Emerald Patrick.

The ensuing confrontation between Gordy and Elizabeth over his time spent at Ruby's was ugly. She initially forbid him from setting foot in the café. Gordy honestly explained that he simply went there for breakfast. He admitted that it was nice to have someone interested in what he had to say and what was going on in his life. Amazingly, Gordy was able to shame Elizabeth into relenting, as he framed her as a paranoid and uncaring wife, which was the truth. Despite the reprieve from Elizabeth, he knew that it was best to cut back on his time in Ruby's.

In typical Gordy fashion, he didn't have the initiative to tell Emerald why he had cut back on his visits to the café. Eventually, Emerald found out from a friend that Elizabeth had become suspicious of the two and a big fight had ensued. She was hurt, as she looked forward to her daily banter with Gordy. In recent weeks, her mood perked up as Gordy began to come in to Ruby's on a more frequent basis. Emerald felt sorry for

Gordy, but she sensed that he was covering up some dark things in his life. She assumed that it was his family life. Little did she know that his work world was spinning out of control with no good outcome in sight.

As was their custom, Barry County Sheriff Buford Blakeley and Ernie Lambert, Prosecuting Attorney for the county had to have a good lunch as a part of any serious discussion. Their favorite eating spot was Ruby's Pancakes and More.

Blakeley was in charge of the investigation into the explosion, even though it wasn't being deemed as a crime scene. He knew that due to the extreme level of property damage and the presumed loss of life, the potential for insurance claims and lawsuits was off the charts; especially when someone like Elizabeth Blanchard smelled money. When faced with situations like this, Buford Blakeley always leaned on his friend Ernie Lambert for advice.

Ernie Lambert was in his tenth year as prosecuting attorney for Barry County. His career and his stature in the Bouvier community were transformed early in his tenure as prosecutor when he led a rape investigation that identified then Bouvier Chief of Police, Jack Buggle as a rapist. Until the time of the courageous investigation of Chief Buggle, Lambert had been seen by most Barry County patrons, and by Lambert himself, as an overweight, lazy, and underachieving attorney. The investigation of Buggle drastically changed the public's view of Lambert. Most importantly, it also transformed the underachieving Lambert into one of the most highly respected prosecutors in Southwest Missouri. For most of his professional life, Lambert had tipped the scales at more than 275 pounds on his 5' 6" body frame. As his self esteem improved, so did his physique. Lambert lost over one hundred pounds and was clearly a different person, both from a physical and attitude standpoint.

Despite having a healthier perspective, Lambert couldn't resist a trip to Ruby's for the daily special, especially when he was stressed. Today was clearly one of the most stressful days in his professional and personal life. Gordy Blanchard had been a long-time friend of Lamberts.

Their visit to Ruby's got off to a rocky start when they found out Emerald wasn't working. Ernie swore he saw a tear come to Buford's eye when he found out that Emerald wouldn't be there to wait on them and have their usual banter. Buford was hungry and needed some home cooking as soon as possible, even though his portly physique spoke volumes that he could miss a few meals without harm prevailing upon his body or health. The last time Buford had weighed in, approximately three years earlier, he was mortified to see the numbers 328 displayed on the screen of the medical office scales. The doctor treating Buford at the time strongly encouraged him to get into some type of weight loss program. Buford agreed and was committed to the health initiative until around noon that day when he heard that Emerald was serving barbecued ribs, corn on the cob, corn bread, and blackberry cobbler for her daily special.

The lunch mood turned around when Buford heard the waitress speak the heavenly words, "smoked brisket." He and Lambert ordered the brisket specials accompanied with fried potatoes, green beans, and peach cobbler for dessert.

Sheriff Blakeley then got around to discussing what he had witnessed and learned so far that morning. Ernie Lambert clearly understood that his friend was nervous about leading the investigation of the explosion and having to assign blame or a cause for the terrible tragedy. From a political standpoint, pointing blame at one of the more power entities, Bouvier School System, the City of Bouvier, Barrco Energy, or the natural gas company; would create enemies in areas that you normally didn't desire if you were a sitting politician in Barry County. This was why he greatly desired the assistance of someone accomplished in dealing with delicate matters. In Barry County there was no one better suited to assist Sheriff Blakeley than Ernie Lambert.

After Blakeley went over the various scenarios of how an explosion of this magnitude could occur, Lambert brought up the option that Buford didn't want to even contemplate at the moment. What if Gordy accidently caused the explosion? Or what if Gordy intentionally caused the explosion?

Buford shook his head and said, "Ernie, I will look at everything at the crime scene and make an honest judgment. But you and I both know, if it were to point to Gordy screwing up in some damn way, I will be crucified for tarnishing the legacy of a good guy who died too damn soon."

"I know, Buford. I'm just trying to cover all the possible ways this might have played out. You know, it's probably something we can't even comprehend at the moment."

"Like what, Ernie?"

"Maybe there was a tremor from the New Madrid Fault and it created a leak in the gas line. Stranger things have happened."

"Or my luck, it's something really strange, like you said, something we can't comprehend right now."

"Let's eat before we get even more depressed than we already are today."

Around this time Lambert and Blanchard could hear the conversations taking place in the nearby tables at Ruby's. What they heard made both realize, this was going to be an extremely delicate task.

As is the custom with the death of a person in the prime of their life, Gordy Blanchard's life as a slacker was quickly forgotten and rewritten as word traveled around the community about his tragic death. Praise for Gordy came from all corners of the business and education sectors of Bouvier. The common phrases heard around the community were, "He held so much promise. Oh what an outstanding and ambitious young man that has been taken from us." And the most disingenuous, "He was so much like his dad. In fact, Gordy was probably going to be a more dynamic leader for Bouvier than Milford had been."

After overhearing the sympathetic talk about Gordy, Lambert came up with the idea to put the Bouvier Fire Chief Leroy Boulevard in front of the media to handle the initial round of inquiries about the fire. This would give Sheriff Blakeley the opportunity to conduct his investigation without the blinding light of the media shining on his every move or spoken word. The Sheriff thought it was a great idea as long as the Chief didn't say anything embarrassing or stupid. He knew Leroy much better than anyone and he had seen the best and worst of Leroy Boulevard. If Leroy followed his script it would be a great idea, but if Leroy had to answer any questions, 'Lord help us,' was the thought going through Sheriff Blakeley's head.

"Now keep in mind, Ernie, you don't know Leroy like I know Leroy. If he has to answer any questions, no telling what he might say."

"I understand, we will give him a prepared statement and then you can reinforce to Leroy that he is to answer no questions from the media under any conditions. When in doubt he should say, 'We cannot comment on an ongoing investigation at this time.' Do you think he can stick to that type of script, Buford?"

"If he is on a short rope, Leroy will do fine. I will give him the talk."

Lunch concluded with the Sheriff going forward with their plan. Despite the process in place, he was worried about what his days ahead foretold. His concerns centered around the various constituencies that he would be dealing with and possible outcomes impacted by his results. To help mitigate his worries, Buford ordered an extra peach cobbler, to go, topped with vanilla ice cream for good measure. As he walked out of Ruby's he had a momentary smile on his face. It was a beautiful pre-fall day with the sun hitting the Bradford pear trees in the parking lot of Ruby's. Buford thought, 'If only the circumstances in Bouvier could be as bright as today's sunlight.'

After spending an 18 hour day walking through the ruins of the former office of Gordy Blanchard, the Fire Marshall's initial conclusion was the explosion erupted from a crack in the natural gas line running into the heating system to Gordy's office. Toward the end of the day, they came upon what appeared to be a wedding ring and then they found a Bouvier class ring lodged on a burnt piece of bone fragment. The year engraved on the ring was the same year that Gordy Blanchard graduated from Bouvier High. With those two pieces of evidence, sheriff Blakeley was able to declare that Gordy Blanchard had perished in the explosion.

Chapter 4

Per the plan put into place by Ernie Lambert and Buford Blakeley, the front man for discussing the initial cause for the explosion was Bouvier Fire Chief, Leroy Boulevard. Leroy was clearly enjoying the attention as head of the biggest fire investigation in recent memory for the Bouvier community. With the inspection of the explosion site complete, the TV crews showed up from Springfield and Joplin and Leroy couldn't wait to discuss the preliminary cause of the explosion. Standing 5'4" and over 280 pounds, Leroy was a memorable figure on the local TV stations reporting of the Bouvier School explosion. His wife made him wear a tie for the big media event, but the only problem was that Leroy's dress shirt had been purchased when he weighed at least 40 pounds less than his current portly figure. The TV reporters were seriously concerned that Leroy was in danger of chocking from an apparent lack of oxygen and or blood supply to his head, due to the severely tight shirt collar and equally tight necktie. Nevertheless, Leroy managed to make it through his initial press conference without choking; however he did say something he would later regret.

As Leroy was about to end the press briefing, he uttered that he found it hard to understand why a gas line would suddenly leak when no construction work had been conducted in that area of the campus in decades. When pressed for more information, Leroy became irritated, red faced, and said, "Hell if I know, makes you wonder if it wasn't intentional," and stomped out away from the reporters. Leroy's takeaway line created more and more questions from the locals and the media than the Bouvier Police or Fire Departments were prepared to nor wanted to answer. Those questions added to the myth and lore of the deceased Gordy Blanchard.

Upon hearing Boulevard's utterance, Lambert wanted to personally choke Leroy with his tight necktie. As soon as the press conference was over, Lambert summoned Boulevard and Blakeley into his office and gave Leroy the tongue lashing of his life. Ernie Lambert rarely lost his cool, but this September day was one of the few times he felt justified. After a few moments of hearing Lambert's tirade, Leroy Boulevard had heard enough. He stood up, with his face even redder than it was in the press conference, pointed his chubby finger at Ernie and Buford, and said, "I've heard enough of your bull shit. You two pant loads can take this investigation and cram it up you asses as far as I'm concerned." He pointed at Buford and said, "The next time those damn reporters want to come to town, you can trot your happy ass out there and you'll see how much damn fun it is."

The next thing Ernie and Buford saw was the sight of the portly Leroy Boulevard pushing a reporter before jumping into his pickup truck, peeling his tires, and throwing gravel as he made his get away from the Bouvier Courthouse area. One reporter caught Leroy's exit on videotape and it was included in the TV station's story about the fire explosion investigation.

Many in Bouvier were upset about the manner in which the town was portrayed by the TV stations. The one person most upset was Ernie Lambert. His plan to keep the investigation going smoothly without the bright glare of the media had backfired miserably. He sensed at that moment that Leroy's comments were a bad omen, but he had no idea what might be next to crop up in the investigation of Gordy Blanchard's death.

By the time of the official declaration of his death, the Blanchard family had already started to make peace with the fact that they would never see Gordy again, but hearing those words from sheriff Blakeley were gut wrenching in a way one can never explain or be prepared for until it happens.

As Buford left the home of Gordy and Elizabeth Blanchard, Milford Blanchard sat in the same chair he always frequented when visiting Gordy. Only this time he wasn't talking to Gordy about a football game on TV or a golf match earlier in the day. He became overwhelmed with emotions that he hadn't felt for years or decades. At this moment, Milford T. Blanchard felt as if everything he had held to be true had been wiped out.

Since the day that Gordy was born he had envisioned Gordy growing up in Bouvier, going off to get an education and then coming back to Bouvier to start a career and eventually a family. Despite the various setbacks Gordy had encountered in his personal and professional life, Milford had never let go of that dream for his little boy, Gordy. Now after hearing the final, chilly words from Buford Blakeley his dream was over, broken and shattered, as was Milford T. Blanchard.

A strong person can only take so much and on this September day Milford T. Blanchard had met his match. His wife could tell that her husband was destroyed by the blank expression on his normally impressive face. Nancy Blanchard had never seen that look in her husband's eyes before. Of course they had seen their fair share of disappointments like any other couple or family, but Milford had been resilient beyond compare. This was much different and she immediately thought, 'I wonder if Milford will ever recover from this?

Only one other time had she seen him look beaten and that was when his pastor Durwood Hardy disclosed an infidelity in his life. The breach of trust by his pastor was stunning and took several months for Milford to regain his normal self after those events unfolded.

The sight of Gordy's blue pickup truck parked in the administrative parking lot was buried in Milford's mind. He kept asking himself why Gordy was intent on going to work so early on a Sunday morning in September. He would never know the answer, but it continued to nag at him.

Milford knew that Gordy was worried about the upcoming audit of the school finances. Now he was racked with the thoughts that he should have done something to help him out. He continued to think that if he offered Gordy some assistance with the audit, then maybe Gordy wouldn't have needed to go in to work early Sunday morning.

Milford couldn't imagine any type of wrong doing on Gordy or anyone else's part with regards to the school's finances. He was worried that Gordy was overwhelmed with the finance side of his relatively new position and had probably made a mistake or two due to inexperience. Had Gordy been afraid to ask for help out of fear of looking weak?

Milford knew that Elizabeth had hurt Gordy's self esteem with her verbal lobs when the prior year's audit came out. He had heard the cold harmful things that Elizabeth had said throughout the school about Gordy that were framed in a way to make herself look good by comparison. But the one concern that had continued to be on the forefront of Milford Blanchard's mind wasn't Gordy's ability to do his job or his focus on his job; it was Bre Pattone, the accounting manager for the Bouvier School District.

Bre Pattone joined the Bouvier School District five years earlier to assist in the accounting department of the Superintendent's office. Over time she moved up and became the accounting manager reporting to the Assistant Superintendent. Bre's accounting and organizational skills weren't her only valuable assets. Bre was also very attractive. She was a little over five feet eight and sported a figure that would catch the attention of practically any man within her sight. She was 40 years old with jet black hair and a pair of rather large surgically enhanced breasts. In fact her first boob job was such a success for Bre in capturing the attention of men in the Bouvier area that she went back to get another enhancement four years later. Bre's attire usually included a tight fitting blouse, which showed either a small or very healthy amount of cleavage, depending upon the occasion or her needs at the moment.

Bre's successful work skills didn't carry over to her ability to stay married. She was a four time divorcee and was in hot pursuit of husband number five. Bre's first husband was her high school sweetheart with whom she had her first child at the age of 18 during her senior year in high school. That marriage lasted for two years until Bre was caught with her old high school volleyball coach in a cheap motel near Roaring River State Park. Marriage number two was to her high school volleyball coach, Fletcher Salisbury. Unfortunately for Bre, Fletcher was quite fond of many of his former players. Marriage number two ended with Bre catching Fletcher and a seventeen year old from his volleyball team in the same motel that had ended Bre's first marriage.

The first boob job enabled Bre to reel in a businessman from the lake community of Castle Rock for marriage number three. That marriage lasted for another three years until Bre became infatuated with her daughter's boyfriend, Trey Handsbrough, who happened to be the quarterback of the Bouvier football team. One fall evening after a big

Bouvier football victory, Bre met up with Trey in town and showed him her appreciation for his outstanding play in the game that night. The only problem was that Bre's suspicious husband had the entire event, which lasted just over 94 seconds, video taped by a private detective who had been tailing her for the prior couple of weeks. Bre's nearly two minutes of passion with Trey Handsbrough ended marriage number three and her relationship with her daughter Destiny.

Marriage number four was the shortest and for Bre the most traumatic, which considering her track record, was saying a lot. She married Ellsworth Jameson, who was rumored to be a wealthy retired insurance executive, less than a year after she blew up marriage number three. Ellsworth was 25 years older than Bre, quite handsome, and very popular with the ladies. He had moved to the area a year before meeting Bre, so he had not been privy to all of her prior marital disasters nor her reputation for being someone with loose morals, to put it kindly. Fittingly, Bre had not done any homework into ole Ellsworth's background.

Ellsworth Jameson was a retired insurance executive, but he wasn't exactly wealthy. He had a beautiful home overlooking the stunning Roaring River State Park, which also had a rather healthy mortgage. Ellsworth's lifestyle of attracting and romancing beautiful women had wiped out most of his retirement cash, but he still had hopes of swinging retirement on his pension from his long-time employer. Those futile dreams went down in flames when he met up with and married Bre. She smelled cash and Ellsworth was eager to make her believe the myth that he was wealthy. Their marriage started off with cruises to the Caribbean and Cancun, a ski vacation in Colorado, a European venture, and finally a weekend stay in New York City.

The cash had long ago run out, so Ellsworth started skipping a mortgage payment or two to make the vacations as fun as possible. Just as Bre was planning a trip to the California wine country, she found out that Ellsworth's lender had started foreclosure proceedings on their home. She was livid and the ensuing fight over foreclosure news was ugly. Ellsworth was hit with the full Bre storm of vengeance. In the midst of her tirade, Bre saw Ellsworth become silent and clutch his chest. Within the next couple of minutes it became apparent that he was having a heart attack. Bre called 911 for an ambulance, but before the paramedics could arrive Ellsworth's condition worsened. Bre was going nuts. The news of the foreclosure and now Ellsworth's medical condition had her in a moment of panic. She knelt down over Ellsworth and began to cry and yell all at once. She screamed out, "How did this happen, why, why, why?"

Before he took his last breath, Ellsworth looked up at Bre, who was looking very hot in her signature V-neck blouse, which showcased her ample cleavage. He smiled and said, "But you have to admit, the sex sure was great." As the paramedics came rushing in, Bre sat there stunned as she realized that Ellsworth had died sporting a full erection.

Ironically, Ellsworth the retired insurance exec had failed to change the beneficiary to his life insurance policies after his previous divorce. Upon finding out that she stood to inherit nothing of value from horny ole Ellsworth, Bre had him cremated without the benefit of any memorial service.

Six months after his death, the mortgage company that had financed Ellsworth's beautiful home completed the foreclosure of the residence. By this time, Bre had moved out, but the bankers discovered one remaining item when they took possession of Ellsworth's home. Ellsworth's ashes were in a cheap urn sitting on the fireplace mantle. When the banker contacted Bre to see if she wanted Ellsworth's ashes, she replied, "Yeah, I've got a low spot in my driveway that needs filled. Just dump them there whenever you get the chance."

Chapter 5

As the sun rose over the skies of Northern Arkansas, Gordy Blanchard anxiously contemplated this new life that lay ahead of him. The plan for his new life had been thoroughly pieced together, but Gordy was still nervous. As he drove past the rice and cotton fields, he was filled with mixed emotions about his new fate. Driving a car that had been placed for his getaway, Gordy was excited about his fresh start - free from his mistakes and any preconceived notions about his capabilities.

Like any rational person, he was nervous about moving away from the only place he had ever known and the only life he had ever lived. He had developed a close relationship with Emerald Patrick, owner of Ruby's Pancakes and More, over the past few months, and even though is wasn't an affair, he felt like he and Emerald had a special connection.

Gordy had grown up in Bouvier and other than four years at Missouri State University, he hadn't lived anywhere else. Because of this, he kept having to remind himself that he had no other choice than to run to start a new life.

Gordy Blanchard had long realized that Bre Pattone was bad news. The depths to which she would go to achieve her wicked dreams wasn't fully known to Gordy until a few weeks earlier.

From the moment that Gordy was promoted to Assistant Superintendent, Bre Pattone had set her sights on appealing to him, which wasn't so bad at the time. The flirtations became more and more overt and clearly Bre could tell that Gordy was enjoying the attention. She had heard the rumors about Elizabeth Blanchard and Elizabeth's uncaring manner for Gordy. She also became keenly aware that Gordy was in way over his head in the financial aspect of his position. Gordy continually had to rely upon Bre to assist him with even the most basic financial overview functions of his job. With this knowledge, Bre pounced upon an opportunity to play upon Gordy's weaknesses.

Even though he initially had no proof of any financial wrongdoing on her part, Gordy developed a looming sense that Bre was manipulating the school financials to her benefit. The more he became suspicious, the more he tried to distance himself from her flirtations. Sensing that Gordy's attitude was changing toward her, Bre upped her game to build ammunition if she were to ever need to blackmail Gordy for her own personal benefit.

Gordy's suspicions were correct. Bre was stealing from the Bouvier School District and doing so in a big way. To make matters worse, she was working her financial magic in such a way to make it appear that Gordy Blanchard was the one doing the pilfering of the school's books. As an additional insurance policy to protect herself from Gordy ever turning over any discovery of wrongdoing to authorities, Bre was quite ingenious in adding an element of blackmail to her arsenal of dirty tricks.

On a few occasions, Bre had let her flirtations go too far and while doing so, Bre had made sure to get her actions photographed. On one occasion, she came into Gordy's office, snuck up behind him and kissed him without wearing a blouse or bra on her shapely body. She then proceeded to place her rather large cleavage in front of Gordy as she kissed him again. As Gordy tried to push Bre away, his hands touched various exposed parts of her attractive body. Bre's photos of this exchange gave the impression that Gordy was in fact fondling her for his own sexual pleasure.

Bre's behavior had totally caught Gordy off guard. She had always been flirtatious, but this was crossing a line and he had not seen it coming. Before he could get up and remove himself from Bre acting like she was in heat, Bre came at Gordy and wrapped her arms around him and kissed him like she had never kissed a man before. Her cell phone had been used to video the whole event. The still footage of a partially naked Bre kissing Gordy would be worth a lot to Bre if she were to ever need to extort anything to her benefit from Gordy.

Gordy finally was able to excuse himself from Bre and her very large surgically enhanced breasts. He stood up and asked Bre to leave immediately.

"Bre, what the hell are you doing? Are you out of your mind? Get some clothes on and never do this again. It's totally inappropriate."

"Gordy, I'm so sorry. I just thought you needed a little encouragement. You've seemed down lately."

"Bre, I appreciate the thought. But if you want to encourage me, please do so with all your clothes on and with no romantic gestures. My God, I'm married and I'm your boss. This would have looked horrible if someone had walked in when you were acting like you were in heat."

"Gordy, like I said, I'm sorry. This won't happen again. You have my word."

"God, I hope so. Let's go back to work and act like this never happened."

The level of Gordy's embarrassment led Bre to see that her actions had hit the intended mark. Gordy was very concerned about the appearance of any impropriety. She knew he would be easily blackmailed, if the situation were needed.

As Gordy entered the farming community of Brinkley, Arkansas, he realized that this would be his best opportunity to fill up his vehicle with gas. He also felt that it would give him an opportunity to get his mind off of Bre Pattone. He chose a small gas station that he was confident wouldn't have any type of video surveillance system. It was an old Sinclair station that was having a hard time paying for soap for the restrooms let alone affording a video camera system. He pumped the gas and went to the restroom while wearing a large golf hat and large black sunglasses, which were typically worn by professional fishermen. He paid for the gas, a large bag of pretzels, and a Diet Coke with his new credit card that had his new name, Gordon Blansford. The same person who had helped him obtain the getaway car had assisted Gordy with the new credit card and name. He was relieved when the gas purchase went through without a hitch.

Gordy suspected that the explosion would consume the Bouvier community and wouldn't create any doubts about his death, but he didn't want to take any chances. Thus the need to use remote locations for gas, large hats, and sunglasses. As he got back into the car, he figured he would probably need to get gas one more time before he reached his destination, Seaside, Florida.

The next step of his plan was to expose Bre Pattone and her wicked plans to defraud the Bouvier School System. Heading East on I40, Gordy felt lucky to be alive. Surviving the explosion wasn't the only reason he felt this way. After Bre made her sexual overture toward Gordy, he was perceptive enough to realize that he was in way over his head in many ways. He knew that he didn't have the necessary skills to properly do his job. He also knew that he was dealing with an immoral person who was going to manipulate his weaknesses to her advantage. That's when he made the phone call that more than likely saved his life.

Blair Jennings was born and raised in Bouvier, Missouri. She and

Gordy were babies together in the nursery at the Bouvier Lutheran Church and had been best friends all their lives.

Blair went to Missouri State University with Gordy and was a four-year letterman for the MSU Volleyball team. She was Captain her senior year and led the Bears to the NCAA Volleyball national semi finals. Her incredible play enabled her to be named first team All American, which was the first time an MSU Volleyball player had attained such an honor. After graduation from MSU, Blair went on to obtain a master's degree in Finance at the University of Florida. From there she worked in corporate finance for three different Fortune 500 companies before starting her own hedge fund. The combination of her brilliant mind and unbelievable determination propelled Blair to tremendous success in the complex world of hedge funds.

Blair was a striking beauty. She was six feet tall with long blonde hair and a killer physique. She had been Gordy's first love. They had never dated in high school, as they had a relationship that could be characterized as best friends.

Once away at college, Gordy decided he would see if there was more to their relationship. He confided to Blair his real feelings for her and as he finished, Blair broke down. She was moved by Gordy's heartfelt love for her, beyond that as a best friend or a big sister. It was then that she confided to Gordy that his words meant more to her than he could ever imagine, but she was a lesbian.

Blair asked Gordy to keep this a secret until she was ready to go public with this part of her life. As they hugged and cried, Gordy promised Blair he would honor her wishes. In fact, they shared an apartment together for their final two years at Missouri State. They possessed a bond that many happily married couples would envy. That gave Gordy some level of satisfaction in not being able to be romantic with Blair, but deep down, he still loved her like he would have if he were her husband.

Months earlier when Gordy reached out to Blair, he informed her that he was in deep trouble. The more Gordy confided in Blair the worse the situation appeared to her. Gordy knew that anything he told Blair would never be repeated. He desperately needed the brutally honest viewpoint of someone who possessed the objectivity that he needed. Living nearly 900 miles away from Bouvier gave Blair the ability to see things much clearer and objectively. The more Gordy confided in Blair the more she became concerned, not only for Gordy's future as a free man, but also for his personal safety.

Blair realized that Gordy was in no way shape or form prepared to take on someone as cold, conniving, immoral, or smart as Bre Pattone. She immediately contacted, MZL & Associates, a private detective firm she had used several times to conduct research for her business. Once she relayed the basics of Gordy's plight, Mac Z. LeGarge, owner of MZL swept into action. Mac Z. LeGarge was a retired Air Force Colonel who formed his firm after a distinguished military career. Blair had met him through social interactions at the Hurlburt Air Base, which was near her home in Seaside, Florida. She often wondered if Mac had really been in the CIA, due to his extensive travel history. Over the years he had become a dear friend, one with whom she had the utmost respect.

From the balcony of her stately beachfront home in Seaside, Florida, Blair stared at the beautiful sunrise coming up over the Gulf of Mexico and wept as she realized the magnitude of Gordy's situation. Mac Z. LeGarge's initial scan of Gordy's computer at the Bouvier School

District revealed many grave problems, which were serious violations of the law. There were bonuses paid to Bre Pattone each month, which in turn were not being reported to the school's board of directors. Additionally, there were wire transfers to a suspicious appearing vendor. Further research unearthed that the vendor, Rocko Limited, LLC, was solely owned by a sketchy character named, Rocko Gorski. The more MZL & Associates looked into Gorski, the more concerned LeGarge became.

The brief summary that MZL could come up with on Gorski wasn't good news for Gordy Blanchard. Bre Pattone had started dating Rocko Gorski approximately nine months earlier. Gorski owned a fitness gym in Bouvier. He prided himself as a former professional boxer who had once gone Mike Tyson 10 rounds when Tyson was on his way up in the professional boxing circle. His claim was a bold faced lie, but the more Rocko told it the more he began to believe the exaggerated tales of his past. Most of his adult life he had served as a bouncer at bars and strip clubs and as an occasional muscle man for groups with mob ties in Kansas City and Tulsa. This is where Rocko's resume became dark. He served three years in prison at the medium security facility in Farmington, Missouri for drug trafficking and unlawful use of a firearm. After his release from prison he moved to Bouvier. Living with his cousin Ridge, who allowed Rocko to move in as long as he remained drug free, refrained from partying, and had no run-ins with the law.

Despite his checkered past, Bre Pattone was immediately infatuated with Rocko Gorski. One of his strong points was his ability to capture the attention of the ladies. He had jet black hair that was slicked back in a style made famous by basketball coaching great, Pat Riley. He stood 6'4", weighed 235, and had a physique that always made women look twice when he walked by. Rocko's confidence and swagger sealed the deal for Bre, plus she loved the naughty boy aspect of Rocko. The more she learned of his street smarts, the more she realized that Rocko would be the perfect accomplice to pull off her desired big haul from the Bouvier School District. This became even more evident when she realized that one of the skills Rocko had obtained while in prison was money laundering.

The plan she began to hatch was classic Bre. She could benefit financially by manipulating Gordy Blanchard's computer log-in, funnel money for her benefit but without ever having her finger prints on any of the wrongdoing. Rocko's fictitious business would receive the money, which would originate from Gordy's computer file at the school.

The monthly bonuses paid to Bre were illegal. The fact that they were never officially approved or disclosed to the Board of Education was an even more challenging legal point for Gordy. As her plan unfolded, Gordy was the person responsible for disclosing such payments and obtaining approval. Also in accordance with her plan, Gordy had no idea any of this was going on under his authority. So far, Bre's elaborate scheme had successfully escaped Gordy's detection, which wasn't hard in light of his limited curiosity, and his even more limited accounting and managerial capabilities.

Mack LeGarge's team quickly put together the basics of the Bre plan. The next step was to find out what was being communicated between Bre and Rocko. Mack feared that Bre's association with a thug like Rocko was going to lead to a bad ending for someone and he suspected that it was probably going to be Gordy.

Mack's assembled team was able to place a bug on Bre's phone and a tracking device on her school computer, which allowed them to monitor every keystroke. Gaining access to Rocko's phone was a greater concern for Mack's team. However, they way overestimated Rocko and his protection mechanisms within his gym. A female member of Mack's team visited Rocko's gym, inquired about their hours, classes, and workout regimes. Rocko took the bait, as expected. He immediately began to cozy up to her and lost all interest in his cell phone. Within 15 minutes she had been able to place a bug on his phone and one in his office cubicle, which looked over the workout area of his gym. Rocko's computer was the next target, but it wasn't visible during her encounter with Rocko.

The next step was the most important. They had to gain access to Bre's home. Careful observation of her home provided their best access point. This time it was Rocko who once again came to their rescue. Their observation of Bre's home revealed that while Bre was working and scheming at school, Rocko was providing personalized training for a teenage customer at Bre's home.

For two straight days Rocko snuck a shapely young lady into Bre's home. After the first time, the MZL team made their way into Bre Pattone's home undetected while Rocko and the young lady were rocking the upstairs bedroom. The team placed bugs in Bre's bedroom, kitchen, and master bath. They were able to exit the property, once again just as Rocko and his young client were getting dressed after their quite vigorous private workout.

The next few hours of surveillance provided shocking details for the MZL team. This required a plan of action to save Gordy Blanchard, not only from a professional and legal standpoint, but more importantly for his personal safety. The decision was made by Mack LeGarge and Blair Jennings that they should jointly discuss the findings of the MZL team with Gordy as soon as possible.

Blair reached Gordy on his cell phone while he was working at school. She tried to sound as calm as she could under the circumstances, but she had to convey to Gordy that he needed to be extremely serious about what Mack was going to discuss with him. He agreed to call Blair as soon as he could leave work.

Approximately fifteen minutes later, Gordy Blanchard placed the phone call that more than likely saved his life. Blair conferenced in Mack Z. LeGarge and he began to explain what his team had discovered. Mack began his presentation in a calm manner that was made even easier by his deep southern accent and a slow cadence that came with his life as a true southerner and career of providing briefings for people such as General Norman Schwarzkopf and at least three U.S. Presidents. Gordy immediately discerned that he liked the guy and could trust him, even if he was nervous as hell.

"Gord, I have to be totally blunt and honest with you, bud. You are in a real pickle. Bre Pattone has put you in danger professionally, legally, and personally."

Gordy politely interrupted when he heard the word, personally.

"Colonel LeGarge, you said personally, what do you mean, sir?"

"Gord, this chick is really bad news and she has teamed up with a greasy, gel haired thug named Rocko Gorski. Rocko is an ex-con, who appears to have learned a few things during his time in prison. Specifically, he gained the ability to assist with money laundering among other skills. They have a plan and Bre has been executing the plan under your nose. She has manipulated your school computer. Payments are being made to Rocko Limited, LLC, without board approval and bonuses are being paid to Bre Pattone each month, also without board approval. In other words, Bre has hung you out to dry from a legal standpoint. You appear to be a lone wolf paying unauthorized expenditures to Bre and her boyfriend."

Gordy interrupted, "Colonel LeGarge, I didn't do this. There is no way in the world I would have done anything without the approval of the Bouvier School Board."

"Gord, I understand, but you allowed your computer to be manipulated by Bre Pattone. Therefore, you are negligent, even if it can be proved that she did this, which is going to be a tough thing to prove. Negligence isn't going to save your ass. It might lessen your prison sentence, but it will still get you fired."

"Did you say prison? Did I hear that correctly?"

"Unfortunately, Gord, you are in a real tight spot legally, thanks to this Pattone woman, but that part of the story is the lesser of your worries. The other part of their plan is to kill you."

"What? Kill me? Why?"

"Based upon what I've been able to pull up so far, the money wired so far to Rocko, LLC is small potatoes compared to what they want to pull off. The first wires were just to see if their plan could work. Now that they know they can do this, undetected by you, they are going to go for the financial home run, so to speak. They plan to initiate a multi million dollar wire transfer to Rocko Limited, LLC. Then they are going to kill you and dispose of your body in your office. After that, Rocko is going to detonate an explosion to give the appearance that you died in a gas line accident. This will divert attention away from their money laundering. Thus giving Bre and Rocko time to leave the country with several million dollars courtesy of the Bouvier School District."

Mack Z. LeGarge paused for a moment to let his comments sink in with Gordy. The conversation immediately went silent as Gordy tried to grasp the details of what he had just been told. He didn't know what to say. His mind was numb. Finally, he uttered the words, "What should I do, Colonel?

In his slow southern accent, Mack replied, "Gord, I'm glad you asked. We have a plan. I'm just not sure if you will like it. We can make you disappear, but the manner in which you disappear is up to you. If we make you disappear, we can expose Bre and Rocko, and save the school's finances, but it's more complicated if you don't. Understand, there is no way I can protect you from being killed if you stay."

Chapter 6

The legendary Durwood Hardy had seen and heard many problems in his three decades as pastor of the Bouvier Lutheran Church. He had also seen his fair share of mistakes made by people, whom he never dreamed would proceed down paths that would later end up in heartache and despair. He was also one of those who had taken these paths himself, so he keenly understood how good people could make terrible mistakes.

The discussions he had been having with Gordy Blanchard had greatly distressed Reverend Hardy to the point that Durwood was having difficulty sleeping because of his concerns for Gordy. What concerned Durwood the most was his realization that Gordy felt hopeless in his professional and personal life. Gordy was careful not to divulge details of his professional situation, but Durwood was certain that Bre Pattone was more than likely a major source of Gordy's anxiety at work.

As a pastor in a small town, Durwood Hardy was in the position to hear a lot of things that most people wouldn't be able to obtain. Bre Pattone had been a subject of more stories involving lust and breach of trust than any other person in the scandalous town of Bouvier. The fact that she worked with Gordy greatly concerned Reverend Hardy. Even though Gordy never mentioned Bre by name, he suggested that he was being manipulated by someone at work. When Durwood asked Gordy to describe the level of manipulation from 1 to 10, with 10 being the worst, Gordy reluctantly said it was at least a level 9.

Durwood Hardy desperately wanted Gordy Blanchard to reach out to someone for guidance for how to get out of his situation. The week before the explosion, Gordy let it slip that "it may be too late to right the ship." Durwood Hardy was floored by Gordy's clear sense of hopelessness.

As Gordy Blanchard headed east on I49, near Hattiesburg, Mississippi, little did he know of the chain of events beginning to unfold in his beloved Bouvier. Within the next few days, the scene of the explosion would be examined thoroughly to find out why it took place and to try to find whatever remained of his body after experiencing the horrific explosion.

Driving down the highway gave him a lot, probably too much time to consider and contemplate whether any mistakes were made by himself and the MZL crew in the days leading up to the explosion and his presumed death. The mistakes he had made in his job were embarrassing enough, but to be exposed while trying to escape would be unbearable. The explosion was much greater than anticipated. The thought of people in Bouvier finding out that he was responsible for inflicting horrible damage to the school where he received his education and his employment was something he hoped would never see the light of day.

The other thing that he was having difficulty getting used to was not being able to call his best friend, Chad McMasters. He and Chad had grown up together in Bouvier. In fact they were also babies together in the nursery at the Bouvier Lutheran Church. They had been best friends for their entire lives. Not a day went by without them talking on the phone or dropping by to see each other at work. When traveling, a call to Chad was part of Gordy's routine to pass time on the road or to laugh about something or someone witnessed along the way. Gordy was also missing Emerald Patrick. Their daily talks and banter at Ruby's Pancakes and More were fun and kept him going during the darkest moments. They didn't have a physical relationship, but Gordy knew he was in love with Emerald.

Now he had no one to call except Blair Jennings or Mack LeGarge. In order not to arouse any suspicions or undue attention, he had been instructed to only call in the case of an emergency until he safety arrived at Seaside, Florida. So that meant killing time by listening to the radio and people watching along the interstate. To make matters worse, the car provided for him was too old to be equipped with satellite radio. So there were no sports radio stations to help Gordy pass the time on his route to Florida. There was also another area Gordy had been warned about. Colonel LaGarge had drilled into Gordy the practice of avoiding eye contact while driving and at any stops along the way. The Colonel had impressed upon Gordy the fact that many times he had seen fugitives captured in part because of eyewitness accounts after coming into contact or seeing the person in passing. As he approached his way into Hattiesburg, Gordy obeyed orders and kept his cap low and his shades on as he got ready to stop at a Circle K store on the outskirts of town for a much needed bathroom break.

Chapter 7

It was decided that the funeral for Gordy Blanchard would take place on the Sunday following his presumed death. The hope was that an entire week would help absorb the trauma of Gordy's death, but in reality, for many of his close friends; it would take much more than a week to get over the shock of his passing. The family had tried to reach out to as many of his old friends as possible. They quickly found that social media outlets were proving to be incredible resources in getting the word out about his demise in the violent explosion.

Over the objections of Gordy's father, Milford T. Blanchard, the legendary Durwood Hardy would be conducting the service. Despite his near sainted status, the senior Blanchard was in the distinct minority of people who despised the Reverend Hardy. Milford T. Blanchard was one of the leaders in the Bouvier Lutheran Church when Hardy came forward with the news that he had fathered a child out of wedlock twenty-one years earlier. While the majority of the congregation forgave Hardy for his sin and admired his courage to come forward with the news, Milford T. Blanchard was never able to forgive Hardy. Despite the disconnect between the senior Blanchard and Hardy, Gordy Blanchard remained close to Reverend Hardy and was a regular attendee of his church.

The Reverend Durwood Hardy had conducted many funerals of young people during his tenure at the church. He keenly understood how difficult and emotional it was for family and friends to lose someone in the prime of their life. But preparing for Gordy's service was one of the most gut wrenching times of his career. He had been close to Gordy. When things weren't going well or if he just needed someone to talk to after a stressful day, Gordy always knew he could count on Durwood Hardy to be there for him. That is precisely why Reverend Hardy felt so helpless months earlier when a very despondent Gordy Blanchard came to him for counseling. It was the first time he had ever seen Gordy appear to be on the verge of hopelessness. Despite his best effort, he couldn't get Gordy to open up about what was going on in his life that would push him to the depth of despair that he was experiencing.

Playing the "what if" game was something that Durwood Hardy rarely, if ever, did in his personal or professional life. However, looking back on his conversations with Gordy Blanchard prior to his death, it made Hardy wonder if the incident leading to Gordy's death was really what it appeared to be; an accident. Reverend Hardy hadn't uttered a word of his doubts to anyone, but he had an inner voice telling him that questions needed to be asked in order for the investigation to be proper and complete. He keenly understood the need to ask any questions delicately and to be careful to whom they were broached.

The meeting with the family to prepare for the service was something Durwood wasn't looking forward to on this beautiful September day. Luckily for him and all concerned, Milford T. Blanchard chose not to attend the meeting. The family said he wasn't feeling well, but Durwood knew better. It wasn't a secret that Blanchard couldn't tolerate being in the same room with the highly revered Hardy, so when he made the decision not to attend the meeting, the entire family was relieved.

The next obstacle for Durwood was going to be Elizabeth Blanchard. He laughed with his wife earlier in the morning when he said, "The meeting would be much easier to plan for if I knew which Elizabeth was going to show up, the crazy and rude Elizabeth or the nice and calm

Elizabeth." Since the meeting was going to include members of the Blanchard family, he was hopeful that the nice Elizabeth would grace the room today.

Luckily for Reverend Hardy, Elizabeth was in a good mood. Her mood had been helped due to the fact that she had just learned that Gordy owned two life insurance policies. Gordy's parents had purchased one of the policies and the other had been purchased by Gordy just a couple of months earlier. She was frankly shocked that Gordy had any life insurance. In all, Elizabeth stood to haul in over $750,000 from Gordy's untimely death. She was already making plans about booking appointments with realtors in Florida for a gulf front condo.

Durwood Hardy welcomed everyone into his beautiful office in the Bouvier Lutheran Church. Before sitting down behind his large semi circle mahogany desk, Hardy offered all the guests some of his renowned Costa Rican coffee. Nancy and Elizabeth Blanchard were accompanied by Elizabeth's parents, Phil and Carmella Grace.

Nancy Blanchard had never cared for the Grace family. They had made their money in the last decade and were more than a little too rough and pretentious for her tastes. Carmella, who spent way too much time in the tanning bed, had a strange orange tint to her skin, which drew everyone's unwanted attention. Nancy Blanchard, however, conducted herself with consummate grace and class despite the circumstances. Elizabeth was dressed in a little black dress, which was much tighter and shorter than Nancy Blanchard felt was becoming for a grieving widow meeting with a pastor to plan a funeral service for a deceased husband.

The meeting started off with a short prayer by Reverend Hardy, which seemed to help take the stress and tension out of the room. He then began with the usual questions for the family, which pertained to their initial wishes for hymns and bible verses. Things were going well, in fact much better than he expected, until Hardy asked whom they wanted to deliver the eulogy. At this point Gordy's mother interjected that she and Milford thought it would be fitting for Baxter Flynn speak from the standpoint of someone who knew Gordy as well as anyone and had very supportive of him professionally. Milford had made it known that having the Superintendent of the Bouvier School System speak was a must for his son's service. He understood more than anyone the level of respect afforded to the school superintendent in Bouvier.

As soon as the mention of Baxter Flynn speaking at the service was broached, Durwood Hardy could tell that a nerve had been hit with Elizabeth Blanchard. She became red faced and immediately crossed her arms in a manner befitting a child acting like a spoiled brat. At this point Hardy decided to face the inevitable problem head on. He paused for a moment, leaned forward, and asked, "Elizabeth, are you ok?"

The question caught her off guard, for a moment, but just when everyone thought she wouldn't respond, Elizabeth began to cry.

"I just have to say, I'm not comfortable with Baxter Flynn speaking at the service."

This clearly surprised Nancy Blanchard. Before she could respond, Elizabeth started talking again about her feelings regarding the Baxter Flynn idea.

"Baxter Flynn? Really? Why would anyone seriously think that would be a good idea? Let me tell ya, Baxter Flynn would love to be able to march in front of the big crowd and talk about how he and Gordy were such good friends, and he would actually make a lot of people think it was true. But Baxter Flynn doesn't deserve the honor of speaking at Gordy's service. Just saying!"

As soon as Elizabeth Blanchard stopped rambling, the room was filled with silence and it was one of the most uncomfortable moments Durwood Hardy had ever witnessed. He deliberately let the silence set in for longer than Elizabeth Blanchard wished. She put her head down, knowing full well that she had stepped on Nancy Blanchard's toes, in a major way.

To ease into a discussion and not a full-scale confrontation, Hardy decided to ask Elizabeth some questions in order to clarify and hopefully diffuse the tense situation.

"Elizabeth, please tell us why you feel Baxter shouldn't speak at the service. Tell us your specific concerns about this choice."

Elizabeth was clearly flustered. She started to clam up, but over her best instincts she began to babble on about Baxter Flynn.

"I guess I shouldn't hold it against him, but Baxter has the job that Gordy should have had. Gordy should have been the Superintendent of Schools, not Baxter Flynn. Baxter put Gordy in the Assistant role and set him up for failure. Gordy wasn't an accountant and everyone knew it. That's what killed him."

A very frustrated Nancy Blanchard couldn't help herself from being silent any longer. As calm as she could be under the circumstances she interrupted Elizabeth.

"Elizabeth, we think the world of Baxter Flynn. He promoted Gordy and treated him well from everything Milford and I could see. Everyone, except you, could see that as much as we wanted him to have the job,

Gordy wasn't ready to be Superintendent yet. He needed more experience and that's why Milford recommended that Gordy go for the assistant job."

"Of course you did, Milford liked it that way."

Nancy Blanchard wasn't happy with that retort. "Elizabeth, what exactly do you mean by that statement?"

Elizabeth clearly realized that she had really messed up by challenging the Blanchard's. So she did what she knew best, she decided to play the emotional victim. She began to cry uncontrollability. "Nothing, just nothing. I don't know what I'm saying. I'm just so upset about losing Gordy. I just wish I could feel like I had some say in planning his service."

The meeting had clearly taken a turn that Durwood Hardy wasn't expecting. Over the years he had maintained a good relationship with Nancy Blanchard, despite her husband's hatred toward him. He sensed that Nancy was more than capable of handling the situation, if she were given the unrestrained opportunity to speak directly with Elizabeth. At this point, Durwood, gently interrupted Elizabeth's painfully loud and fake sobs, "Nancy and Elizabeth, would you like us to give the two of you some time to talk things over alone?"

Nancy Blanchard gave Durwood a pleasant smile and a nod. "Reverend, I think that would be preferable at the moment. Thank you very much. We will let you know when we are finished with our discussion."

Elizabeth Blanchard wasn't expecting this turn and did not want to have to face Nancy Blanchard alone, especially after the way she had just conducted herself. Her face turned pale and the giddy thoughts of condos in Florida were now far removed from her mind.

Durwood stood and motioned for Elizabeth's parents to follow him. They didn't know whether to go or stay, but Phil Grace stood and took Carmella by the hand as if to say, 'Let's get the heck out of this room before things get any worse.' Phil was red faced and clearly embarrassed by his daughter's actions. He mumbled that she was starting to act more and more like her mom, before realizing that Carmella was close enough to hear anything he might say. Luckily for Phil, the sobs from Elizabeth drowned out any rude mumblings coming from his lips.

Nancy Blanchard gently closed the door to Durwood Hardy's office. As she began to sit down in the seat that she had occupied from the start of the meeting, she noticed Elizabeth stand up and begin to pace the room. Elizabeth had a strange look on her face that immediately caught Nancy's attention. As Nancy began to speak she noticed Elizabeth had her arms folded and was staring at the beautiful carpet in Hardy's office.

"Elizabeth, please tell what is going on today? I have to admit, your behavior has me puzzled. I know you are hurting. We all are hurting and will continue to be in a fog or state of shock for quite some time. Frankly, your attitude toward Milford and me is hard to believe, hurtful, and rude. I don't care how much you play the sympathy card. I won't tolerate being treated this way, especially after I've lost my boy. I hope you can pull yourself together so that we'll be able to make the arrangements for Gordy's service without any additional drama or stress."

Elizabeth stood motionless for several seconds and then began to sob uncontrollably.

"Nanc, I'm sorry, I truly am. I guess you get stressed and then begin to lash out at those closest to you. I don't know how to express this without hurting you and Milford, but I'm not sure Gordy is dead. I can't put any thing specific on why I feel this way, but I just do. It's driving me crazy.

I'm about to collect on life insurance and plan a funeral service for someone that I have this sixth sense is still alive."

Nancy Blanchard was more than startled by Elizabeth's words. She immediately thought about family members who had lost loved ones in the 911 terror attacks. Those same people had to make peace with the fact that they would never have the certainty of finding the body of their deceased loved one. They simply had to move on and find closure in other ways than burying the body of their family member. She could tell that Elizabeth was genuinely panicked about not having the closure she needed and wanted in a time like this. Elizabeth then mentioned this strange feeling she had recently been having.

"I don't know exactly why, but I feel like I'm being watched. I can't pinpoint an exact person, time or date; but I just have this eerie feeling that someone is there."

"I have read where people, who lose someone in a manner like Gordy's death, have a feeling that their loved one is watching over them. Is that it?" Nancy asked.

"I've read that as well. But this is different, because I sensed this weeks prior to Gordy's death. In the last few weeks Gordy was very stressed and he clearly wasn't himself. I would swear that our house was being watched prior to his death. There was one guy who I would see drive by the house and he wasn't someone who lived in our neighborhood."

"Did you mention it to Gordy?"

"Yes, initially he didn't seem concerned about it. But the more I discussed it I sensed that it was something he didn't want to talk about. I just chalked it up to Gordy being busy and his mind on his work and the upcoming audit."

Hearing this concerned Nancy. It made her wonder what was going on in Gordy's work situation prior to his death. Ironically, the talk did give her some relief in knowing what was causing Elizabeth's behavior. She was concerned that Elizabeth would need some professional help to assist her with the mourning process, but Elizabeth would resist, believing that she could handle anything on her own will and intelligence.

Nancy leaned over to Elizabeth and gave her a hug. "You know we are in this together. Don't feel like you have to handle this situation on your own."

At that moment, there was a gentle knock on the door. It was Durwood Hardy. He was half expecting to be serving as an intermediary when he knocked, based upon how the meeting had been going, but he was startled when he saw the Blanchard ladies embracing.

"I'm sorry to interrupt. Do the two of you need some more time to talk? "

Elizabeth looked up with a smile, while tears rolled down her cheeks. "No, no, Reverend, we are fine. We are ready to continue. "

From that point on the meeting went well. The service was finalized without any additional confrontations or drama. At the end, Elizabeth requested one additional speaker to give a perspective of growing up with Gordy. She asked Durwood to contact Blair Jennings to see if she could come to the service and speak about being Gordy's best friend while they grew up in Bouvier and their time at Missouri State University. Nancy Blanchard loved the idea. She and Durwood admired Blair and knew she held a special place in his heart. Little did they know what kind of role Blair was still playing in his life.

Durwood Hardy knew Blair Jennings from her time growing up in Bouvier. In fact, his daughter Caroline Hardy had remained close to Blair after she moved to Florida. He was confident that he would be able to make contact with Blair, with Caroline's assistance. Durwood told the Blanchard's that he would be in contact with them once he confirmed everything with Baxter Flynn and Blair Jennings. The meeting concluded with a short prayer.

After the meeting was over, a relieved Hardy called his other daughter Mary into his office. Mary served as his associate pastor. She enjoyed hearing the recap of the meeting. Normally Mary would sit in on the meetings of this nature, but she had little regard for Elizabeth and Milford Blanchard. She had seen them in action and was not a fan. Before he left his office, Durwood told Mary, "I sincerely hope the service on Sunday can conclude without any additional drama. Despite my personal feelings for Milford Blanchard, he deserves a special day to recognize the life of his son, who was a really good guy. Gordy was a little lazy, but a sweet kid."

"Dad, why is it that you have to call anyone under the age of 40 a kid?"

Durwood chuckled and gave his daughter a peck on the cheek as he headed out of his office.

Chapter 8

Gordy's drive to Florida was especially difficult because it caused him to sift though his mind the events and mistakes that led to the decision to save his life and his reputation. The other thing that was tough was not being able to do some of the things that had been important in his life. One of these events was not being able to see his beloved St. Louis Cardinals as they headed down the stretch for another division championship. As he was making the drive he realized that he and his buddy Chad McMasters would have been getting ready to head to St. Louis to see the Cardinals play their rivals, the Cincinnati Reds in a crucial Central Division series. As he entered the city limits of some small town in southern Mississippi, Gordy checked his wallet to see if he still had his tickets. The sight of the Cardinals logo was tough to see. As he drove a few more miles, he pondered the thought of turning around and heading up I55 and making it to the games.

The thoughts going through his mind were, 'Hell, I don't have any schedule to keep right now I'm dead. I might as well go.' His spirits were lifted when he saw the first positive to being dead. A dead Gordy can do anything he wants to do, but then he settled back to reality and thought about Blair Jennings and Mack LeGarge. They had done so much planning to get him safely out of Bouvier; he couldn't turn his back on their plan. They would be livid if he decided to turn around and head to St. Louis. He could just hear Colonel LeGarge lecturing him about all the bad things that could result from such a deviation from their plan.

As Gordy was pondering his decision of whether to head to St. Louis, Mack LeGarge and his team were preparing for the next round of attacks on Bre Pattone. With Gordy safely out of the picture, they had a great deal more latitude with regards to Bre and Rocko. Their surveillance would be the key to making a case against Bre. The initial recordings after Gordy's death provided an interesting mix of what Gordy had been dealing with in the days leading up to his "death."

The news of Gordy's death stunned Bre Pattone. She and Rocko immediately got into a huge argument over what they should do next.

"Great, Rocko, now what are we going to do? If you had done what you were supposed to do we would be in possession of our money and out of here. I sincerely hope the explosion wasn't your fine work. It would be like you to do something stupid like that."

A livid Rocko wasn't about to take this lying down. "What the hell do you mean, 'if I had done what I was supposed to do?' I had a plan. How the hell was I supposed to know that the bastard was going to get blown up?"

"You know exactly what I mean. You were supposed to kill Gordy. I had the money ready to go. But you got preoccupied with your gym. How do you get so busy with a gym at this time of the year?"

"You are such a dumb bitch. The explosion wasn't me. The dumb bastard was in the wrong place at the wrong time. Bad luck happens to people. I had a plan. You act like doing a job on someone like this Blanchard dude is a piece of cake. You get haphazard and you go to jail. I had my plan. The time wasn't right. Everything has to be lined up just right. The time, the place, the assistance, and most importantly, the place for the body have to be lined up perfectly, so that it won't be discovered. And you definitely don't blow up a building at six in the morning. God, you're a dumb bitch. Holy crap do you remember talking about any of this?"

Bre wasn't in the mood to be called a bitch or anything else. But being called a dumb bitch by a greasy prison thug like Rocko was something she wasn't going to tolerate. The emotion resulting from the thought of possibly losing out on millions of dollars combined with Rocko's attitude sent her overboard. The next thing Rocko saw was a twelve inch pampered chef carving knife within inches of his crotch area. Bre was incensed and Rocko's family jewels were soon to be her target.

Mac LeGarge and his team thought they were about to hear a murder take place. It wouldn't have been the first time for them to hear such an event, but all prior operations were in the pursuit of Al-Qaeda terrorists - not a large breasted bimbo and a greasy thug.

After all the screaming and yelling ended, LeGarge wondered if anyone was alive. He desperately wished he had a surveillance camera in place to capture what had just gone down at the Pattone residence. Their recording devices picked up the sounds of Bre as she began to clean up the mess from her fight with Rocko. To escape her testicle targeted wrath, Rocko planted his left fist firmly on her right cheekbone. When she came to, Bre realized that Rocko was gone and she had blood dripping from her face. She realized that they better make up and come up with an alternative plan fast or her dream of living in Belize with millions courtesy of the Bouvier School District was going up in smoke.

The LeGarge team was amazed as they heard Bre ranting and raving around her house. It became clear to them that Bre was alone because no other voices were interacting with her. That wasn't stopping her from having a conversation, even though it was with herself. Bre was game planning and going over all types of alternative ideas. She was discussing things that were going to be a treasure trove to LeGarge and whomever decided to relay his findings. Bre's biggest concern was getting access to her school computer and, in turn, Gordy's files. Despite her declarations to Rocko, she wasn't even remotely close to being ready to kill Gordy and embezzling millions. The off-shore accounts to house her treasure trove weren't set up. Plus, she had not decided how she would take care of Rocko after they pulled off the heist.

All of these ideas and problems were being poured forth for LeGarge's team to record, and they were relishing the opportunity to capture every single word. Conveniently for them, Bre was in the room that had the most microphones and she was standing incredibly close to one of the devices. The quality of reception was outstanding. Their luck couldn't have been any better when they placed a call to her cell phone, posing as a DirecTV repair tech. By answering the call in the manner in which she did, she would place herself without any possible way of denying that she was the person on the recordings by LeGarge's team.

"Bre?"

"This is Bre"

"Is this Bre Pattone?"

Yes, this is Bre Pattone, who is calling?.......

"Mam, this is Carlton, with DirecTV, we are following up on your requested service call."

"No, you must have a mix up, I have not requested a service call

"Mrs. Bre, is your address 1004 Mill Creek Rd?"

"No, my address is 1411 Mill Creek Rd....."

"Very good, Mrs. Bre, I apologize for the mix up. Have a good day."

Mac LeGarge and his team were very pleased with their work for the day. They realized that their surveillance of the Pattone residence wasn't over. In fact, in many ways it was just getting started because they keenly understood that Rocko Gorski would be back. Bre needed him and she always got her way with any man within her sights.

Mac LeGarge was pleased that his initial plan was going exactly per his playbook. Gordy Blanchard was safe, away from Bre Pattone and Rocko Gorski, and LeGarge hoped that Gordy was following his detailed instructions for the journey to a new life in Florida.

The next step would be a tricky dance with the local prosecutor, Ernie Lambert. Not surprisingly, LeGarge had done his homework on Lambert. He had found that Lambert was what he typically found in prosecutors in smaller counties. He was a very good prosecutor, who knew the law, and was smart in his administration of his prosecutorial targets. He definitely wasn't a blow hard trying to make a name for himself at the expense of potentially innocent people.

Ernie Lambert was known as someone who could sort through all of the facts and make a solid, common sense decision, without regard for who was involved in the case. He was clearly someone that LeGarge couldn't intimidate or push around based upon LeGarge's extensive background in military intelligence.

LeGarge wanted to establish a connection and inspire some curiosity in Lambert, but he wasn't ready to turn the whole case over to him yet. Once all of the pieces to his plan were in place, he would divulge more to Lambert. His initial meeting would be more of an appetizer than a full meal.

Chapter 9

Raleigh J. Calhoun had practiced law in Bouvier for several decades. He was the sole practitioner at The Calhoun Law Firm, the most prestigious law firm in Barry County. A child of the south, Mississippi to be exact, Raleigh was a true southern gentleman. Over the years he had become acquainted with the Blanchard family, though he wasn't what you would call a family friend. His wife, Charlyn Belle, and Nancy Blanchard had been long-time friends. Because of his level of prestige, trust, and family connections, Gordy Blanchard had sought out Raleigh J. Calhoun prior to his death.

Raleigh was in his early sixties, slightly overweight, and had a beautiful full head of gray hair, which gave him quite the dashing look. He still caught the eye of women around town, but he was totally devoted and faithful to his beautiful and elegant wife of thirty-nine years, Charlyn Belle Calhoun.

The news of Gordy's passing had hit Raleigh hard. He pondered what he should do with his knowledge of what Gordy had shared with him for a few days. At first, Raleigh felt as if Gordy's secrets should die with Gordy. Hopefully few, if any others knew of Gordy's mistakes. However, the more he contemplated the situation, the more he felt moved to share his knowledge with someone whom he could trust. That person was Ernie Lambert.

Gordy Blanchard had not provided Calhoun with all of the sordid details of his situation. Calhoun was quite sure of that. But the desire to protect Gordy Blanchard's name from being tarnished in death and the need to place Bre Pattone on the radar of the local prosecutor led Calhoun to call for Lambert to come by his office.

Ernie Lambert was a trusted friend to Raleigh. In fact, Raleigh had helped mentor Ernie when he came to Bouvier. So, when one received a call to drop by the law office of Raleigh J. Calhoun, you didn't blow off the request. In fact, most astute attorneys would be in his office within the hour. That was certainly the case for Ernie Lambert on this beautiful fall day in Bouvier.

Ernie loved getting the opportunity to sit down with his friend and he greatly admired Calhoun's office. Raleigh had a strong liking to the Southern colonial designs, and it clearly showed in his law office. He had by far the most impressive law office of any attorney in Bouvier. This was partly because he was the most successful of his legal brethren in the town, but also because of his sense of Southern style and culture. Being a child of the South, Raleigh never let go of his love of things southern - even though he had lived in the Ozarks of Southwest Missouri for over thirty years. He had come to Bouvier because his wife, Charlyn Belle, was from the area. Over time he grew to love the unique way of life in the Ozarks, but deep down, Raleigh longed to be in his beloved Mississippi.

Raleigh warmly greeted Ernie and motioned him to sit in one of his plush leather chairs. Ernie knew something important was on the agenda. He had known Raleigh too long and could sense when he had something other than college football or some juicy gossip on his mind.

Raleigh started things off by talking about the outpouring of sympathy for the Blanchard family and the sense of loss within the Bouvier school community.

"You know Ernie, not only did we lose Gordy but we also lost a building that was a big part of the Bouvier school heritage. Hell, that building was built by the WPA crews during the Great Depression. People are really down right now."

"I know, Raleigh, its hit the town hard. Everyone liked Gordy. Granted, he was seen as a slacker by many, but who could argue that he was genuinely nice and caring."

"And when someone dies at a young age, all of their flaws disappear and are temporarily forgotten. That's the case right now with Gordy," Raleigh stated.

Ernie knew right then that Raleigh was easing the conversation toward Gordy Blanchard. The next question going through his mind was, 'why?'

Raleigh adjusted his red and white tie and rubbed his chin before he continued their conversation.

"Ernie, before he died, Gordy Blanchard made an appointment to see me, which frankly surprised me. Gordy had always been a good kid and had never needed legal advice, except when he purchased his home. I drew up the contract for that transaction, but that was the only other time Gordy had been in my office.

He came in and I could immediately discern that the boy was in some type of trouble."

Ernie leaned forward and interrupted Raleigh.

"I'm sorry, Raleigh, but you said Gordy was in trouble?

"Yes he was in a real mess. His tit was in a wringer as we like to say back home."

"At work or at home?"

"Work. Well, from what I've heard and observed, I'm sure his home life was hell too, but Gordy was in a real mess a work."

Ernie paused before he ventured any further into his inquiry with Raleigh. He respected Raleigh way too much to leap into any assumption that was unfounded, but he could clearly see Raleigh wanted him to know something and it was important.

"Raleigh, am I safe to assume from this discussion that Gordy was privy to wrongdoing at the school?"

Raleigh grinned and as he tried to suppress his trademark infectious laugh, he just couldn't. His beautiful red and white tie moved in concert as his laugh became more pronounced.

"Ernie, I'm sorry. Yes, poor ole Gordy had been manipulated worse than a rented mule. Before I go any further, let me ask you this, do you know a Bre Pattone?" As soon as he asked the question, Raleigh knew the answer by the smirky grin on Ernie's face.

"Yes, I've heard of Bre Pattone. I've never had the pleasure of meeting Bre, but she has quite the reputation around Bouvier."

"You know Ernie, I have never met the lady either, I probably should not use that term for her, as Charlyn Belle would definitely not be happy. She has a few other terms to describe Ms. Pattone, as any southern lady can do when talking about someone with the moral make up that Bre possesses."

Ernie laughed and added, "Yes, my wife calls her the town slut."

Raleigh liked that one and joined in, "Charlyn Belle one day saw her in town and called her the "bimbo on steroids." I guess she was referring to that massive boob job she received from one of her numerous ex husbands."

"Raleigh, I try not to give unsolicited advice to my colleagues in town, but when I saw her get promoted at the school, I was concerned. Concerned to the point that I came close to talking to Baxter Flynn about my concerns, then I thought better of it. So, what had Bre pulled over on Gordy? Or I hope Gordy was astute enough not to be having an affair with that slut?"

"Oh, I think Bre would have been more than happy to lure Gord to her bedroom, but at least Gord had the good sense not to go there. Apparently, she tried once and he rebuffed her overture. No, Bre manipulated poor old Gord in other ways. According to him, she got ahold of his passwords and log-in information and was performing financial transactions on his behalf for the school."

"Oh hell! How bad is it?"

"Ernie, I can't answer that because I don't know for certain. Gord knew she was transferring money to a company owned by her boyfriend. I wasn't told the total amount. She was also paying herself monthly bonuses, without board approval, under the appeared authority of Gord."

"Well, does Baxter know anything about this?"

"You are the only person I've told. I presume he doesn't know. He was going to know pretty soon, as they were going to have their annual financial audit in the next month."

Ernie sat in the chair trying to take all of the information in before he began to ask all the questions that were racing through his mind. "So how in the world was Bre concealing this from Baxter and the board?"

"I don't know. Gord and I never had the opportunity to vet that part because he died before our next appointment. But wait, I haven't told you the best part, yet."

"What the hell, Raleigh, there's more?"

"Gordy was convinced that Bre and her greasy boyfriend would eventually kill him to cover their tracks."

"What? How did he know this?"

"For some reason I cannot fathom, Gord was astute enough to hire a big dog investigator when he became alarmed about Bre. The investigator had picked up on a conversation between Bre and her boyfriend, Rocko. That's where Gord got the idea that he would eventually be killed."

"The investigator picked up a conversation; you mean they bugged Bre and this Rocko creep?

"We didn't specifically address it, but I think it's safe to presume as such."

"You've used the term 'eventually be killed' a couple of times. What does that mean?"

"Gordo didn't think Bre was finished with her project. It was only after she and this Rocko creep had completed raiding the Bouvier School's piggy bank that they would kill him."

"But it was going to happen fairly soon, in light of the approaching audit?"

"Because of that, I told Gordy that it was imperative for me to meet with him and the investigator to put together a plan. I advised him that we meet, gather all the evidence, and then come clean with you. It was his only alternative from potentially going to jail and also staying alive. We had to self report this instead of the state auditor finding the violations."

"How did he receive your advice?"

"I thought he seemed to be listening. He agreed to set another meeting date, but I have to admit, I was worried about the boy. I can't put my finger on it, but the boy didn't seem right. I sensed he hadn't told me everything going on in his life."

"We will probably never know now. Knowing this makes his death seem even more bizarre."

"Anything unusual come up so far in the investigation of the explosion?"

"Nothing, so far. Everything points to the gas line. There's more than likely going to be a nice lawsuit against the gas company."

Raleigh grinned after hearing this. He had represented Barrco Energy Gas Company for decades. Defending a case of this nature would be worth a bundle for Raleigh. "Any sign that the explosion was deliberate?"

"Nothing. But it's still rather bizarre to me. Raleigh, before I head on, how do you want me to proceed with the information you've just given me?"

"Like usual, leave me out of it, for now. However, I recommend that you meet with Baxter Flynn ASAP. You might catch him a Ruby's. Today's special is barbecue ribs with blackberry cobbler."

Raleigh and Ernie shared a big laugh and handshake. Raleigh declined Ernie's lunch offer, for obvious reasons. As Ernie headed out of Raleigh J. Calhoun's office he wondered where in the world this investigation would lead him.

As Gordy left Hattiesburg, he thought back to his meeting with Raleigh J. Calhoun. He had always respected Calhoun, in fact more so than any other person, other than his father. The meeting had been suggested by Mack Z. LeGarge as a means to establish credibility for the claims that Bre Pattone had been the person conducting the illegal pilfering of the Bouvier School System. LeGarge had done his research. It had become abundantly clear that Calhoun was the most trusted attorney in town. In fact, he was more than likely the most trusted person in all of Barry County.

Like all small towns, the choice of an attorney was usually filled with four alternatives. Bouvier had a couple of good solid general practice attorneys other than Calhoun. Then there were two talented attorneys who primarily specialized in defending criminal cases such as meth distribution, armed robbery, and a rare murder. Next, were the two or three young attorneys who were getting their practices set up and gaining experience in the legal community. Finally, there were four or five lazy and/or incompetent lawyers who survived merely by happenstance or by having cases dumped in their laps, usually when another attorney had a conflict of interest and could not take the case.

Barry County's legal system had survived with the fourth set of lawyers, just like all other court systems in America. But Barry Countians took a pride in the belief that they more than likely had two of the worst attorneys around. The first was a sole practitioner who was so lazy that it was common knowledge that he was usually asleep on the sofa in the law library in the Barry County Courthouse. The legend of his incompetence was amplified when the trust he wrote for his father was ruled invalid due to several errors in the trust provisions. This resulted in him losing his inheritance due to his own incompetence.

Next, was Rex Moffitt. As a former State Representative, Rex could talk a great game and land some attractive cases. The only problem was he typically lost due to his innate ability to alienate juries against him and his clients from the moment he opened his mouth full of pearly white teeth.

The worst example of this came in a potentially million-dollar divorce trial. Rex was representing the jilted wife who appeared to have a great case after her husband was caught being more than a little too compassionate with his sister-in law less than a week after his own brother's death. After enduring a weeks worth of Rex Moffitt's temper tantrums, the jury awarded his client the princely sum of

$10,001. Afterward the stunned trial judge asked the jury foreman how they derived at such a low figure. The foreman replied, "Every time Rex opened his mouth we deducted $50,000 from his client."

That trial nearly resulted in Rex's disbarment when it was discovered that he had propositioned a shapely female juror during a bathroom break.

Max Z. LeGarge knew from his research that Raleigh J. Calhoun would keep confidential the information provided to him by Gordy as long as Gordy was living. He also discerned that upon Gordy's death, Calhoun would divulge the information in an appropriate and discrete situation. This is what he had learned to love about Calhoun.

As Gordy headed east on U.S. Highway 98 toward Mobile, his mind continued to contemplate his meeting with Raleigh J. Calhoun. The fear of the unknown began to set in and he started wondering in his mind, 'should I have accepted Raleigh's advice and come clean?' He knew going into this decision that this time would come. Mac Z. LeGarge had pounded home the fact that starting a new life wouldn't be all roses and cream. He impressed upon Gordy with the fact that he had done this before for people and the fear of the unknown would set in within the first 24 hours of making the leap. LeGarge said he had even seen people try to change course after taking the irreversible act of starting a new life. Mack had entertained Gordy with his story of literally dragging one poor soul out of the car on the side of I55 near Jackson, Mississippi for fear that the guy was going to head back and interrupt his own funeral.

Mack Z. LeGarge never pressured Gordy into making his decision. He continually said his job was to present facts and options. Mack repeatedly told Gordy that he would respect his decision, regardless of where it took him in life.

Gordy thought back to what Mack had made him do before the MZL team would proceed with the departure plan. He required Gordy to put into writing his reasons for departing Bouvier. Ultimately the departure plan would allow Gordy to remain alive without subjecting himself and his family to the disgrace of allowing the school to be bilked under his watch. Plus, if everything went to plan, the school would be made whole financially.

As Gordy's car approached the small community of Lucedale, Mississippi, his cellphone began to vibrate for the first time in his journey. He anticipated the call to be from either Mack Z. LeGarge or Blair Jennings. However, the caller ID showed that it was a blocked call. He didn't answer, but the call worried him for several miles down the road. He eventually chocked it up as a misdialed number.

Chapter 10

Despite leading two of the highest profile offices in the county, Ernie Lambert and Baxter Flynn had rarely communicated nor had they ever been in a meeting together. That's what made Lambert's phone call more difficult than the obvious. They had no common ground to start with from what would more than likely be a very precarious conversation. Lambert considered various ways of reaching out to Baxter but nothing jumped out to him.

These are the types of conversations that are always difficult and there really wasn't any way to sugar coat it. So Ernie decided to plunge forward. He placed his call to the Bouvier School District, which was in its first operating day out of a mobile home placed in the parking lot next to where the Milford T. Blanchard Administration Building used to stand. He was surprised anyone was answering the phone in light of the total destruction of the administration complex. Much to his surprise, Baxter Flynn wasn't tied up in a meeting.

Lambert couldn't imagine what Flynn's life was like at this moment. He had endured the experience of his best friend and right hand man at school dying in a horrific explosion. He was involved in trying to put the school's administration complex back together, while simultaneously preparing for the funeral of his best friend. And now he's going to hear that his bookkeeper is possibly embezzling money from the taxpayers of the Bouvier School District.

Flynn sounded like someone who was tired and bewildered when he answered the phone. Lambert knew that he needed to be as cordial as possible, but a phone call from the Prosecuting Attorney is usually going to arouse concern. Most people would rather hear bad news as soon as possible. Lambert's experience has shown that drawing it out makes it worse in most instances.

After exchanging pleasantries, Ernie Lambert quickly got down to business.

"Baxter, I can't imagine what you must be going through at this moment. And I hate to interrupt your busy schedule, but I need to meet with you today, if possible."

Flynn sounded even more startled than Lambert had anticipated. "Uh, sure, Mr. Lambert, what does this pertain to?"

"Baxter, no disrespect, but I really need to discuss this in person. Would you be free this afternoon?"

This clearly caught Flynn's attention. "Uh, yes, I guess. Not to be difficult, but I'm sure you can assume that today's not been a good day. I assume it's pretty important or you wouldn't be calling on a day like this?"

"Baxter, you are correct. If it wasn't important I wouldn't interrupt what must be a horrible time for you."

"Do you want to meet in my new office or should I come to your office at the courthouse?"

"I think it would be best for us not to be seen meeting. So let's meet at my office at 1:30 pm today."

A bewildered Flynn could only muster a simple, "Uh sure, that's fine," before closing the call with Ernie Lambert. He was so stunned that he could feel his heart racing. After hanging up the phone, Flynn sat dumbfounded. He put his head in his hands and sat in silence while he contemplated how he was going to move forward. After what had seemed like minutes, but in reality was not more than 30 seconds, Baxter Flynn gathered himself. He was smart enough to realize that Ernie Lambert wasn't calling him to his office to tell him something wonderful. Baxter spoke words to himself that he had used in similar situations, 'I can do this. Whatever comes my way, I can do it. It is God's will.'

Immediately after his short conversation with Baxter Flynn, Ernie Lambert called Sheriff Buford Blakeley. He invited the Sheriff to lunch to get a briefing on the investigation of the school explosion. The Sheriff was on board, especially after he found out that the special at Ruby's was barbecue ribs with blackberry cobbler. Ernie didn't use this conversation to tell the Sheriff any of what he had learned from Raleigh J. Calhoun. Over the years Ernie Lambert had learned that it was always best to tell Buford Blakeley anything important in person. He didn't have any solid proof, but he had his fair share of suspicions that the phones at the Sheriff's office weren't totally confidential.

Shortly before Noon, Sheriff Blakeley ambled into Ruby's. He made his usual trip around the Board of Directors table, greeting and insulting each member of the "Ruby's Board." The Sheriff extended his right hand in an effort to deflect the resulting insults being volleyed back at his direction. Ernie could hear the laughter across the room as Buford did his thing with the good ole boys at the Board of Directors table. Clearly, Buford loved the daily banter with the regulars at Ruby's. Except when it crossed the line of second guessing the performance of his office or when someone said something about his weight, which was a touchy topic for Buford, especially during lunchtime at Ruby's.

Buford was clearly feeling good by the time he sat down with Ernie Lambert.

"Why the hell did you have us sit here? You know I hate this table."

A stressed Ernie Lambert wasn't really in the mood to hear Buford start complaining about the seating assignment at Ruby's.

"Dammit, Buford, did it ever occur to you that I might have chosen this location for a reason? We need to talk. And I mean privately."

"I think someone needs some ribs and in a bad way. So what's up that's so important that we can't sit in the main room? Need I remind you, we get to sittin back here too much and the registered voters sitting in the other room will start thinking we're uppity come election time."

"Ok, Buford. The next time we need to have a private talk, I will have it in my office and have my secretary, Alice, order us some salads from that new fufu joint on 3rd Street."

Buford did a big belly laugh and conceded, "The hell you will. Ok, ok, I'll shut my damn mouth. So what's up, Mr. Prosecutor?"

"I've heard a few stories that are flying around. Any thing come up so far in the investigation of the explosion?"

This immediately got Buford's attention. Just as he was getting ready to reply, the waitress appeared to take their order. Buford jumped in and ordered two specials with one sweet tea and one unsweet tea.

Ernie laughed and replied, "So I don't have a say in my lunch selection?"

"Not on ribs and blackberry cobbler day. When's the last time you didn't order the special? Case closed, Prosecutor!"

Ernie laughed because it was the truth as did the young waitress named Beth. Buford then proceeded to playfully give Beth a hard time, which Beth obviously enjoyed. Buford then asked about the owner of Ruby's, Emerald Patrick. As was the case with nearly all of her patrons, Buford was quite taken with Emerald.

"Where's my girlfriend, today?"

Beth had been hearing the same question all day, but she still wasn't fielding it with her best effort.

"Well Sheriff, uh Emerald isn't feeling well." Beth leaned over and whispered to Ernie and Buford, "Gordy's death has hit her hard. They were close.....if you know what I mean."

There was a long uncomfortable pause. Ernie Lambert was afraid what either Beth or Buford might utter next. He decided to plunge in.

"Beth, please tell Emerald we miss her."

Buford missed the opportunity for discretion.

"So how damn close were they?"

This clearly flustered Beth.

"Oh, it wasn't anything bad. Gordy needed someone to talk to because of his wife and Emerald had always been there for him. It's just so sad. Emerald is concerned about going to the service."

Buford jumped in and asked why.

"Emerald heard that Mrs. Blanchard was jealous of her and all the time Gordy was spending at the cafe. Emerald doesn't want to create a scene or cause any problems with the Blanchard's. They have suffered enough without having to be stressed out by someone in attendance."

Buford wouldn't let it rest. "So when the hell is she coming back? I'd be happy to drop by and talk to her if it would help her out."

"Sheriff, I will let Emerald know you are concerned. Now I better get back to the kitchen with your order or I'm going to get fired."

Buford laughed and yelled, "Make it snappy, Beth, cause Ernie and I are hungry."

Buford leaned back and asked Ernie, "So what the hell were we talking about before that cute little thing came by?"

Ernie just shook his head and uttered, "You know Buford, you really are a sucker for a pretty face. You've honestly forgotten why we were meeting for lunch, haven't you?"

"You know if I wanted an ass chewing, I would have stayed at the office and hung out with that sour puss secretary of mine."

Ernie couldn't help but laugh out loud at the mention of Buford Blakeley's secretary, Pat Gilespi. Pat was known in the court house community as the meanest person on the county's or any local payroll. From a pure knowledge standpoint, Pat, was possibly the smartest person working for Barry County, but she was also mean spirited, back stabbing, gossip spreading, and a devout deacon of her holy roller church in the southern section of the county. Buford has wanted to fire her for years, but she knew way too much about Buford. She was also the niece of the Presiding Commissioner of Barry County. Firing sweet ole Pat would be political suicide for Buford and he has been smart enough to know it. The common joke in the courthouse was that Buford opened the obituaries of the Bouvier Gazette every morning hoping to find Pat's name listed.

"So Pattie has been at it again this morning?"

"Oh hell! She's been on a tear. Someone in the office did something different than she's accustomed to and she went nuts. Hell, we would still be using Big Chief tablets and number 2 pencils to do our jobs if it were up to Pattie."

"Is she still teaching Sunday School at her church?"

"Yeah, and that's another thing about her. You would think she might be a little nicer on Monday and Thursday, the days following her church services. But hell no, she's meaner on those days than any other day of the week. The woman is evil. That's all there is to it. Could we talk about anything but that old bitch? She can put me in a bad mood faster than Ruby's being out of ribs and cobbler."

Ernie laughed and then he leaned forward. "Ok, let's get back to why we called this gathering of the minds, shall we?"

Buford could immediately discern that Ernie Lambert had learned something important. Now he would sit back and see which direction Ernie wanted to lead the conversation.

"So Ernie, anything new on your front?"

"I've been told some troubling information regarding Gordy Blanchard. That's why I wanted to see if anything had come up in the explosion investigation. Has anything come up recently?"

"Nothing so far. Unless we spend some big bucks on a gas line expert, we aren't going to be able to determine exactly why the gas line erupted. So what have you learned?"

"A confidential informant, and I mean confidential, has alerted me to possible wrong doing by Bre Pattone. So to start, tell me what you know about Bre and her boyfriend, Rocko Gorski?"

Buford started grinning at the mention of Bre and Rocko. "Well I can tell you, Rocko is no damn good. So far I haven't been able to collect any proof as to what he is doing. He's a slick bastard; I can see that for sure."

"What do you think he's doing?"

"His name has popped up as someone moving Meth and stolen goods. We've been watching him carefully. So far he hasn't made a mistake that would allow us to make a move on his place."

"What do you mean you've been watching him? This is the first time I've heard about this."

"Calm down, Perry Mason, there wasn't anything to alert you about in this situation. Like I said, so far he hasn't made a mistake."

"I understand, but I just don't want a repeat of the McCelland meth lab case that got thrown out of court."

"I get it, Perry. Are you ever going to stop beating me up over the McCelland case."

"I will stop if you will stop calling me Perry Mason."

This drew a good laugh between the two.

"So tell what you know about Bre Pattone."

"Well the obvious part that we all know is that she is a hot one who will use her body to get whatever she wants, by whatever means she has at her disposal. And man, that last boob job was a stunner. She could turn the head of the most devout Monk. Beyond that, I have been concerned that Rocko has shacked up with her. You take his criminal mind combined with her body, add a dash of her wicked ways, and you have a scary mix there. So what are they up to and how did it involve Gordy?"

"From what I've been informed, Bre obtained Gordy's work passwords and log-in information and was performing financial transactions on his behalf for the school."

"Oh shit! This could be really bad with that much money at her disposal. Do you know any particulars yet?"

"Gord learned she was transferring money to a company owned by Rocko. She was also paying herself monthly bonuses, without board approval, under the appeared authority of Gord. And here's where it really it gets interesting. For some reason, Gord had the initiative and the means to hire a big dog investigator when he became alarmed about Bre. The investigator had picked up on a conversation between Bre and her boyfriend, Rocko. That's where Gord got the idea that he would eventually be killed."

"So the investigator was bugging Bre and Rocko?"

"That is what I have been told. I don't have any information on the investigator, but we need to find them. Do you have any clues on who the investigator might be?"

Buford grinned before he started to answer and tugged on his belt. "We picked up on an out of the ordinary group coming and going in the last couple of weeks. Sometimes it was one guy, a military looking type, and later there were two others who were a bit scary looking. One of the deputies stopped them one day while there was a scene in Bre's neighborhood. They identified themselves as valuators for the State Assessor's Office. They were doing land home valuation audits. The guys had proper IDs that we have seen a million times from the Assessor's Office.'

"I bet those were the guys. Have you seen them this week?"

"Not that I know of, but I will talk to my boys about it. Damn, I can't believe we missed it."

"There was no way to foresee this, Buford, but before you talk to your deputies about this, let's be very careful in what is said to them. We don't want this information out. Nothing. As you can see, this could turn into a major investigation involving massive amounts of money, not to mention, the Bouvier School District. So the boys, as you like to call them, are to know that you want to talk to these guys and nothing else."

Buford never liked being lectured about confidentiality, but he also knew Ernie was right. He knew Ernie always had his back, even when he screwed things up, so he silently took his lecture and nodded in approval.

There was a long pause in their conversation. The timing couldn't have been more perfect for the lunch to arrive. Ernie was amazed to see Buford eat as if he hadn't seen food in years. Ruby's lunch hit the spot and temporarily calmed their nerves. As they finished lunch, Ernie informed Buford that he would be meeting with Baxter Flynn in the next hour to discuss what he had learned about Bre, Rocko, and Gordy. Buford laughed and said, "I would love to sit in on that one. That poor bastard isn't going to know what hit him."

"I know, it's a horrible situation for him. I will keep you posted. And yes, I'm buying today."

Buford loved the sound of that and replied, "You're only doing that because you feel guilty for the lecture."

Ernie laughed, "And for that, today's the last damn time I'm buying."

Ernie smiled as Buford left. For some reason he was confident that Buford would be able to round up the detective Gordy had hired. He hoped his optimism was justified, because this guy could answer a lot of questions and possibly solve some of Baxter Flynn's numerous problems.

Chapter 11

During his long and highly acclaimed career as a pastor, Durwood Hardy had seen his fair share of heart break and despair. No funeral is ever fun to prepare. To his amazement, he had seen a few funerals turn into lively celebrations of the life of the deceased, but the preparation is always tough. Especially if he knew private sections of the deceased's life that he assumed most people didn't know. That always bothered him as he wanted to stay away from a scripture that led in the direction of the failings of the person lying in front of him. Additionally, Durwood would ponder if other members of the deceased's family knew what he knew.

To move past these tough patches, he would go back to the teachings of his beloved seminary professor, Dr. Steven Atson. "No one is perfect. And we shouldn't try to put a spin on their life as a way to preach someone into heaven. That isn't the purpose of the funeral. It is a snapshot of the deceased's life. They probably did some things they weren't proud of, but they also did some really kind and caring things in their life. Talk to the family and friends. Capture the moments where this person made things matter, made things clear, made things bearable, made things fun, and most importantly made someone feel loved. Life isn't always going to be great and it won't always be bad. There will be moments that come along in life that will be fantastic, like the vision of your child learning to ride their bike for the first time. These are the moments where God's grace and glory are shining through a person and making an impact on those around them. Try to capture those moments in the funeral."

The hopelessness that Gordy had conveyed was still weighing heavily on Durwood as he started making preparations for the funeral service. With his thoughts on Dr. Atson, he was looking for inspiration as he sat in his office study at the church. He was hoping for a few uninterrupted hours to put the final touches on his remarks for the service.

Just as he began to make some headway, his cell phone began to vibrate. As much as he wanted to continue his work, it was a call he had to take, Emerald Patrick's name flashed on the display.

Pastors weren't supposed to display preferential treatment, but Emerald Patrick was definitely one of his favorites. Emerald had stumbled into Durwood's life at what was his lowest point and it happened to be the valley for her as well. She had been a wild child -drifting aimlessly until her life came into contact with the Reverend Durwood Hardy. Durwood saw something in her that others had missed and hired Emerald as a secretary at the Bouvier Lutheran Church. This vote of confidence unleashed the potential that even Emerald didn't know she possessed. She flourished in her job. When Ruby's Pancakes and More came up for sale, Durwood and his wife, Veronica, helped Emerald make the purchase. She gave the business a shot in the arm through her spunky, infectious personality. Five years later she is looked upon in Bouvier as a role model especially for girls in Bouvier High School.

Durwood immediately could tell something was wrong. He knew Emerald too well and the tone of her voice was a dead giveaway for him.

"Durwood, I know you are terribly busy with the funeral preparations, but I really need to talk to you."

"Emerald that is no problem. When would you like to come by?"

"I'm headed into town as we speak, how about 5 minutes?"

"That would be great."

As much as he desired to get the message for Gordy's service finished, he could tell that something must be serious for Emerald to request a talk and one so soon. Durwood always desired to get a meeting of this nature completed sooner than later. He hated it when a parishioner would call up and inform him that they needed to talk about a major problem in their life, but then waited several days to actually come by to talk about their situation. In the meantime, Durwood would contemplate and worry about what might be going on in that person's life. He knew he shouldn't do that, but human nature kicks in on this type of situation.

Within what seemed like just a few moments, Durwood's long-time assistant, Francine Asbury, buzzed him to inform him that Emerald had arrived. The next thing Durwood saw was a very distraught Emerald Patrick. He knew her better than anyone other than his wife and he had rarely seen her look this way. Her eyes were puffy, her normally beautiful auburn hair was a mess, and she was wearing a god-awful t-shirt that appeared to have been laundered several weeks earlier. Her trademark perky, slightly cocky persona was nowhere to be found on this day.

Durwood gave Emerald a hug that seemed like an eternity. She wouldn't let go and her sobs became more pronounced. Emerald sat down in her favorite leather chair. It was the same chair she sat in the first time she walked into Durwood's office many years earlier when she was a reckless, aimless, young girl who was in need of direction and someone who would believe in her after she had been raped by the Bouvier Chief of Police.

Durwood immediately handed Emerald a cup of his renowned coffee in hopes of soothing her down so they could talk.

"Em, I'm so sorry to see you like this. Please tell what's happened."

"I will, give me a moment to collect my thoughts. But I need you to promise me one thing before I begin."

"Sure, what is it?"

"That you will believe me."

"Of course, I will believe what you tell me. Why would you think I wouldn't?"

"Well, it's bizarre and I'm ashamed of myself, as well."

"Em, you know I love you and trust you, so don't hesitate to tell me what's on your mind."

"Ok, but before I start, I think I better get another cup of your coffee."

That brought the first hint of the old Emerald as she smiled for the first time since entering Durwood's office. After Emerald poured her cup of coffee, laden with cream, she began her story.

"Gordy started coming to have breakfast on a regular basis. The more I was around him the more I sensed a sadness, a very serious sadness, so I started chatting him up in hopes of making him feel better."

"Did it work?"

"Yes, well I should say, it did somewhat. He started talking to me and started to open up. Gordy had a bad home life, which most people in Bouvier already knew. His wife is an uncaring, social climbing, witch. I hope I'm not stepping on some toes here."

Durwood smiled and said, "You're fine, Emerald, and so are my toes. In fact, they remain untouched." This brought another rare smile from Emerald.

"The more he and I talked the more I came to realize that his home life wasn't his only problem. He hinted that things weren't going well for him at work. One time he said that many days he felt like a failure. I started to cry when he said that. I told Gordy, 'Listen Buddy, you are so young and you are already the Assistant Superintendent of a very well respected school. A failure is the last thing you should feel like.' But he wouldn't listen."

"Did Gordy ever provide any specifics as to why he felt things weren't going well at work?"

"No, he never did. I assumed that most of his darkness was his family life, but I sensed he was keeping something dark from me. Call it women's intuition or whatever name it is when you can virtually read someone's mind."

That got a good laugh from Durwood. "Don't get me started on that stuff."

Emerald grinned, "You know I'm right, Durwood. Gordy would come in early, which I assumed was to avoid the regular breakfast crowd. As I mentioned, over time he warmed up to me."

"I'm totally shocked at that, Emerald."

"Come on, Durwood. I didn't flirt that much. I just tried to interact with Gordy. He seemed so nice and so down to earth."

"So he came in every day for breakfast?"

"For a while and then he stopped. I learned through the grapevine that Elizabeth had become jealous of his breakfast time at the cafe. I'm sure I was spending too much time talking to Gordy and people started talking, like they always do in Bouvier, but I honestly felt sorry for Gordy. He needed someone to talk to and I feel like I'm good at engaging people, making them comfortable and he is very sweet."

Before he proceeded to ask a question that was on the tip of his tongue, Durwood paused, looked up, and asked; "Emerald, you used the present tense when you said Gordy was sweet."

"I know, because Gordy's not dead."

Both sat in silence as Durwood took in what Emerald had just uttered. Emerald began to cry.

"Please hear me out. I'm not crazy and you are the only person I've told or will ever tell that Gordy is still alive."

Durwood calmly reached forward and patted Emerald on the knee, then he adjusted his bifocal reading glasses, just as he does every time he's gathering his thoughts to calm a tenuous situation.

"Listen, Em, you need to talk about what you know, and the last thing I'm going to think is that you're crazy. Obviously, you have information that no one else has and you need to talk to someone, otherwise it's going to wear you down. It's obvious you have to be able to talk to someone you trust, so please take your time, gather your thoughts, and tell me what you know."

"To tell you what I know will expose some things I'm not proud of." Emerald was very emotional at this point. Durwood realized anything he said that gave the impression that he doubted her or was disappointed in Emerald could lead to the conversation ending and possibly hurting his father/daughter type relationship with her.

"Listen, Em, don't ever worry about what I'm going to think about you. You are like a daughter to me. I am so proud of you. We all make mistakes. I do every day. Jesus is the only perfect person to walk this earth. You need to talk about what you know. So do so at ease, not out of worry over what I'm going to think."

"Ok, ok, I appreciate that so much. You're right, I need to talk about this or it's going to eat me alive. Ok, back to where I was. Gordy started coming back to have breakfast and we started talking more. Things never proceeded beyond talking, but I sensed that we were becoming close. I also sensed that Gordy was very troubled. He never gave me specifics but as I said earlier, a girl can tell if something is amiss, so I became curious. Was he seeing another woman, gambling, whatever?"

"When you became curious, what does that mean?"

"It means I basically started stalking Gordy."

"Stalking? Tell me what you were doing that you considered it to be stalking?"

"Well, I was pretty sneaky, because apparently neither Gordy, Elizabeth, nor any of their neighbors caught on to my surveillance of their home and Gordy's comings and goings. I started out watching what he was doing because I was concerned and then it moved into what would best be described as obsession?"

"Obsession? Em, were you in love with Gordy?"

"Yeah, you could probably say that was the case. I really fell for Gordy. The more I was around him the more I couldn't understand why his wife couldn't appreciate what he had to offer. Yeah, he liked to play a lot of golf and fish. But if you had ever been with the duds that I dated back in the day, golfing and fishing are a walk in the park. He's a good guy, handsome, sweet, sincere, funny, hard working, smart, and successful. What more could a girl want?"

"Apparently, it wasn't enough for Elizabeth Blanchard, from the stories I've heard. That's gossip and I shouldn't have said that. That's what I thought drove him to run?"

Durwood paused before he could reply. "Em, did you say Gordy ran? What do you mean by that?"

"I felt like I needed to keep a close eye on Gordy. The days leading up to the explosion he was very down and not like himself. I was worried more than I had ever been about Gordy, so I basically tailed him most of the weekend."

"This past weekend, you tailed Gordy and he didn't know, even Sunday morning?"

There was a long silence. Emerald sat in the leather chair with her head down, sobbing. "Yes, I was following him Sunday morning, and I hope you will believe me because I am telling the truth. I'm not some hysterical girl that can't accept the reality that the guy she fell in love with has died. That isn't the case, at all. You know me too well to believe I could become so weak that I've totally lost touch with reality."

Durwood gently spoke in an effort to calm Emerald, "Em, you know I would never think that way about you. Tell me about Sunday morning. Where were you and what did you see?"

"Gordy left his home early and I followed him to the school. I parked a couple of blocks away, so he wouldn't see my car, since it was still dark. I don't think it was even 5:30 am when he pulled into the parking lot. I watched him enter the administration building and I nearly went in just to have a private talk with him, but I couldn't force myself to do it. And for good reason, because less than 15 minutes later the explosion took place. I was too close to the school and it felt like an earthquake. I was jarred and rocked pretty good; I thought I had been knocked out. But just as I could see through the dust and debris an old car drove by and guess who was driving it, Gordy."

"You saw Gordy drive by immediately after the explosion? How certain are you that it was Gordy?"

"It was Gordy. The person driving the car was wearing the same yellow hoodie that Gordy had on that morning as he entered the building."

"Did you ever see him leave the building prior to the explosion?"

"No, but he told me once about an underground tunnel that ran from his office area to the other side of the campus, which was the same place the old car came from."

"So what did you do after he drove by?"

"What do you think I would do? I followed him some more."

"You followed Gordy? How long and where to?"

"That got real tricky, because I needed gas for my car. So I followed him south of town, while trying not to be exposed. You should try it sometime, its not that easy, Durwood."

Durwood grinned for the first time in quite some time, "I'll take your word for it, Em."

"Fortunately, he headed for Arkansas. I had enough gas to get me to Rogers, before I had to stop. At that point I was afraid I would lose him because he could go so many directions from Rogers. So I guessed he was heading south and guess what?"

"What?"

"I was right. Within 15 minutes I caught the sight of that old car again, so I decided to see how far he was going. He must have had a full tank when he left town, because he made it all the way to Brinkley, Arkansas before he had to stop for gas and a bathroom break."

Durwood needed to rub his eyes and he removed his reading glasses once again. "You mean you drove all the way to Brinkley, Arkansas after a car that you thought was Gordy Blanchard's?"

"No, I didn't stop there, but I got some nice pictures of Gordy pumping gas and leaving the gas station with a bottle of pop and a bag of pretzels."

Durwood sat and stared at Emerald. "You have photos of Gordy Blanchard pumping gas just hours after the explosion at the Bouvier School?"

"Yes, you want to see them?"

"I'm not sure. Yes, yes, I have to after hearing about your journey."

"Oh, it's not over at Brinkley."

Emerald handed her cell phone to Durwood. The first image was the backside of a guy pumping gas wearing a yellow hoodie, and a large golf hat. The next was a side view of the man wearing large black sunglasses, the kind typically worn by professional fishermen, and yellow hoodie walking out of what appeared to be the Brinkley One Stop. The last pic was a front view of the man. The yellow hoodie had "Cubs" embroidered on the front. Durwood sat and stared at that photo for what seemed like an eternity. It had been taken almost 100 feet away, so the clarity wasn't the greatest. Plus the guy in the photo had done a good job to disguise his face, but it sure looked like Gordy Blanchard and the yellow hoodie said "Cubs," which was the Bouvier mascot. As he stared at the photo he almost started to laugh as he thought to himself, 'Only Gordy Blanchard would still be wearing a Bouvier Cubs hoodie while trying to hide from the world. It's classic Gordy.'

Durwood then asked, "Em, you said it's not over at Brinkley. To be honest, I'm afraid to ask what that means."

The spunky side of Emerald began to show up as Emerald continued to describe her journey across Arkansas, through Mississippi, and then into Alabama in pursuit of what was supposed to be the deceased Gordy Blanchard. Durwood sat at the edge of his seat as Emerald described trying to stay close enough to Gordy in his clunker car but sufficiently far enough away to avoid detection.

Durwood interrupted Emerald at this point. He looked at her and said, "Before you go any further, I want you to ask me something."

A puzzled Emerald said, "Sure, what is it, Durwood?"

"Ask me if this conversation is protected by Pastor - Parishioner privilege."

"Ok, Durwood, is this conversation protected by Pastor - Parishioner privilege?"

"Before I answer you, I need to know if you have committed any crimes or participated in a conspiracy to commit a crime in your pursuit of information about Gordy Blanchard?"

Emerald looked puzzled. Before she could say anything, Durwood whispered, "I assume your answer is no, so just say no."

"No I haven't committed any crime nor have I participated in a conspiracy to commit a crime in my pursuit of information about Gordy Blanchard." She paused, and then asked, "What the heck was that all about?"

"It's very important and I will tell you why I asked after you tell the rest of your story. Do you want any more coffee?"

"Definitely! I'll get it."

After filling both of their coffee cups, Emerald continued the story as she reached the outskirts of Mobile, Alabama.

"I guess the hoodie was getting hot, because he pulls into the back of the parking lot at a CVS Pharmacy and gets out of the car to change out of the hoodie into a St. Louis Cardinals T shirt. The adrenaline must have taken over because I just whipped my car into the parking lot and confronted Gordy on the spot."

"Emerald, you are over 700 miles from home and you decide to confront someone you think is Gordy Blanchard? Did you know he was dead at this point?"

"Oh yeah, Facebook was blowing up about the explosion and Gordy's death. Poor choice of words, but yes I knew that everyone thought Gordy was gone. It was bizarre. One minute I'm crying as I read these wonderful tributes to Gordy and the next minute I'm pulling into a CVS Pharmacy in Mobile, Alabama to talk to Gordy. Sometimes you can't make this stuff up."

"So what happened in Mobile?"

"He's getting back into his car and I dial his cell phone again. Not his regular one, but the secret one."

"Secret one?"

"Oh yeah, I forgot to tell you about that. About a week before the explosion he came by the cafe. We were talking for a while and then he excused himself to go to the restroom. I got up to talk to one of my waitresses and knocked over his briefcase. As I was putting the spilled items back I discovered a strange cell phone. It wasn't his regular phone. I quickly scanned the phone details and found the phone number associated with it. That's the number I dialed in Mobile."

Durwood shook his head in disbelief, "Em, I find it convenient that you accidentally knocked over his briefcase."

Emerald gave Durwood a grin that gave a glimpse of the Emerald Patrick that he found to be captivating along with so many others in Bouvier. "Ok, Durwood, let's get back to Mobile."

"Yes, let's talk about Mobile. I can visualize you stomping up to Gordy's car as he's glancing at what you called the secret cell phone."

She loved Durwood's visualization of what went down in the CVS parking lot. "You aren't far off in how it actually went down. As Gordy glanced over to check the phone, I stepped up to the car and tapped on the window. When he turned to see who it was he was stunned, as was I. The big hat and sunglasses were gone. It was Gordy Blanchard."

"It was really Gordy?" said an equally stunned Durwood Hardy.

"Yes, it was and I thought I was going to have a heart attack when I came face to face with him."

"I bet! I bet Gordy was about to have one, as well."

"He was stunned and possibly in shock. He kept saying. 'What are you doing here, what are you doing here?' I started screaming, 'How dare you? How dare you?' He tried to get me to calm down. You know the last thing that a dead guy on the run wants is for someone to call the cops because of a disturbance."

"I've never known any dead guys on the run before today, but that sounds reasonable."

Emerald then became emotional. "Gordy was scared and frantic. He started saying, 'You have no idea what you've done. You may have placed yourself in danger.' I was shocked by his mannerisms."

"What did he mean when he said 'you may have placed yourself in danger?' This is scary, Em."

"I know. I started to calm down and tried to get Gordy to calm down as well. I suggested that we drive to a Starbucks that I had seen down the street, and he reluctantly agreed.

I was afraid he was about to have a heart attack at this moment. He was shaking uncontrollably."

"Did Gordy show up at the Starbucks and did he get calmed down?"

"Yes, thank goodness! I was really worried about him."

"So how did things go at Starbucks? I still can't believe this happened."

"Better and to help you believe this surreal story of mine, take a look at this."

At this point, Emerald handed her cell phone to Durwood and hit play on the video she had selected. The screen initially showed the back of a wall in a Starbucks, but then a person sat down. The person sitting down was wearing a large straw golf hat. The angle wasn't the greatest, but it was clearly Gordy Blanchard. Durwood Hardy was mesmerized by the video. As it played, the thought that kept going through his mind was; 'I'm preaching this guy's funeral on Sunday.'

The narrative lacked substance but it more than made up for it in suspense. There was a lot of crying by Emerald. She rotated from being elated that Gordy was alive to being mad that he had essentially ditched her and all of Bouvier in order to fake his death. She continually kept saying, "If you would give me a reason why you did this I would understand." But Gordy mainly sat stunned saying very little, until he dropped the bombshell on Emerald.

"Emerald, you shouldn't have done this."

"Done what?"

"Followed me here. You shouldn't have done it."

"Why? You know that's pretty funny. You blow up the school, fake your death and you're preaching to me about what I should or shouldn't do."

"I can't tell you what has happened and why things happened because the more you know the more you become a potential target."

"Gordy, what in the world are you talking about? Target?"

"My life is in danger. If I had stayed I was basically a dead man walking."

Emerald began to shake. She couldn't control her emotions. "Gordy, your life is in danger? How? Why? What do you mean? I'm at a loss."

"I made mistakes in trusting someone. I'm no criminal, but some people wanted me dead to finish their scheme. A lot of money is on the line. The kind of people I'm talking about will kill for a lot less than that."

"Are you in trouble with gamblers? I hope it's not drug dealers?"

"No, no, it's nothing like that. I've done nothing wrong except being incompetent and being allowed to be manipulated. You've got to go. Hopefully these people didn't see you or me. Following me will put us both in danger. Trust me, you have to go back to Bouvier and act like this never happened until I get settled."

"Are you kidding me? Go back and act like nothing happened?"

"Yes!"

At this point Emerald is crying uncontrollably to the point it's very difficult to understand what she is saying. Gordy looked sick and very scared.

"Why?

"You and I will be killed if you go back and tell what happened. These people will hunt you down and then use you as bait to get to me. It's that simple. The choice is yours, Emerald."

"Why can't you tell me?"

"If I do, you will be killed."

"What do you mean?"

"I know you so well. You will decide to go after these people and it will get us both killed. These people are pros. You can ask all you want, but this is how it is. We have a plan, but if you get into the mix the plan goes to hell."

"Am I in the plan?"

"Of course, but not until the plan is complete."

There was silence and then it sounded as if Emerald was finally taking no for an answer. She was bewildered, shocked, happy, and hurt all at the same time.

"Answer this for me, Gordy; if I hadn't hunted you down, would I have been in the plan?"

"Yes, Emerald!"

"Liar! How and when were you going to contact me from the grave?"

"We have a plan."

"Who's we?"

Gordy reached into his pocket and handed Emerald a business card. "This guy has put together the plan. If you feel like you are in danger, don't hesitate to call him. Tell him Gordon sent you. But under no circumstances are you to contact him unless it's an extreme situation."

Emerald looked at the card and then asked, "How will I be able to tell if he's one of the people trying to kill you?"

"His name is Mac. He knows the name only I call you. I assume you remember it?"

Emerald began to cry again. As Gordy got up to leave, they hugged and kissed. Emerald whispered, "I hate you and I also love you. You better be true to me, you understand, Gordy?"

"I love you, Emerald!"

"Be safe, Gordy."

"You too, Emerald. I must leave or Mac will be worried."

The video ended. Durwood was emotional and in shock. Emerald was crying again. She softly asked, "What should I do, Durwood?"

"Until I can get my head around what I've just heard and seen, you are staying with Veronica and me. We will contact a security detail from Springfield to discretely patrol our home and the cafe. In the morning we can sit down and decide what should or shouldn't be done, but you have to promise me that you won't do anything that will get you harmed. Ok, Em?"

"Yes, Durwood! Thank you for once again coming to my rescue. I love you, Durwood Hardy!"

"I love you too, Emerald Patrick!"

Durwood gave Emerald a hug before she left. As soon as she was out the door, he collapsed in his chair and immediately began to pray for guidance. He thought he had seen everything in his career; good, bad, bizarre. That was until Emerald walked into his office an hour ago.

Chapter 12

Ernie Lambert really didn't know what to expect in preparation for his discussion with Baxter Flynn. His encounters with him had been strictly in community settings. He wasn't sure if the two had ever really had a conversation beyond the typical, "Good to see you," which is the obligatory insincere greeting of the local elite in social or community settings. When Baxter arrived at Lambert's cluttered office precisely on time, Lambert was caught off guard by his appearance.

Baxter Flynn walked into Lambert's office and gave the impression of someone in a deep fog. Ernie thought Baxter had aged at least 10 years since he had last seen him a few months earlier. His shirt hadn't been ironed and he apparently hadn't shaved since the explosion. Ernie's initial thought was, 'Damn, this guy is in no shape to hear what I need to tell him.' But Ernie also knew that Baxter Flynn had to know what was going on in his office.

Ernie warmly welcomed Baxter into his office and offered him something to drink. Ernie thought Baxter really needed a double bourbon on the rocks, but that wasn't a plausible beverage selection at the Prosecuting Attorney's office. Baxter accepted a bottle of water before Ernie proceeded with the reason for the meeting.

Ernie decided to get right to the point. He had learned that when delivering bad news, sugar coating it usually doesn't help. As soon as you tell someone something negative or bad, anything said to them prior to the bad news is forgotten.

"Baxter thanks for coming on short notice. I wouldn't have called you in this manner if it weren't important."

"Sure, no problem. I have to admit, you've scared the shit out of me. Getting called to the Prosecutor's office is kind of like getting called to the Principal's office in school."

Baxter's comment brought a little temporary levity to the meeting that was already tense. Ernie and Baxter laughed for a short time before Ernie continued his thought.

"Yes, I understand. That's been said to me before. Baxter I'll cut to the chase, I've been told some troubling information regarding Gordy Blanchard. That's why I wanted to talk today. Had you seen anything recently that alarmed you with regards to Gordy?"

"Troubling, alarmed? What the hell are you talking about?" Baxter clearly wasn't in the mood for this type of conversation yet.

"Baxter, a confidential informant, has alerted me to possible wrong doing by Bre Pattone."

"Wrongdoing? Personally or professionally? And how does this pertain to Gordy? Please enlighten me, Mr. Lambert?"

Ernie stuck to the script he had received from Raleigh J. Calhoun. "From what I've been informed, Bre obtained Gordy's work passwords and log-in information and was performing financial transactions on his behalf for the school."

"What? Who told you this, and how long have you known it?"

Ernie Lambert was beginning to dislike Baxter Flynn. "I guess my question for you is, is this true?"

"What do you mean, is this true? This is the first I've heard of anything like this."

Ernie leaned forward and uttered, "And why does that not surprise me? You know Baxter; I was trying to do you a favor by giving you a heads up and to possibly save you the embarrassment of an investigation in a very public way. But from your sorry attitude, I can tell you are taking this about as seriously as your review of the finances at the school. As far as I'm concerned this meeting is over. I'll be seeing more of you in the future.

Baxter Flynn had definitely met his match. It was time to start groveling if there was any chance of salvaging any thing from this meeting. "Mr. Lambert, how about we start over."

"For starters, it's Ernie. Where would you like to start, Baxter?"

"Ok, what information do you have that ties Gordy and Bre?

Being the smart ass, Ernie continued, "Very good question, Baxter. Here's the scoop, Gord learned Bre was transferring money to a company owned by Bre's ex-con boyfriend, Rocko Gorski. Are you familiar with Mr. Gorski?"

"I've seen him around the office a few times. Rough and greasy dude. What do you mean transferring money? School money?

"Yes, school money."

"How much and how do you know this?"

"We don't know. As I said, Gordy talked to a confidential informant prior to his death."

"Were you aware that Gordy discovered that Bre was paying herself monthly bonuses?"

"Monthly bonuses? What the hell are you talking about?"

"So I am assuming from your questions that Gordy never informed you that this was going on inside your office."

"Ernie, I'm confident that there is some mistake. The Board of Education approves all payments at the monthly board meeting. I've never seen a bonus to Bre Pattone on the list of payments."

"I'm confident you didn't see any because Bre was bypassing the board and had manipulated Gordy's computer log-in to conduct her transactions under his approval."

"Gordy didn't have the authority to approve bonuses."

"Exactly! How could this be pulled off without you knowing?"

Baxter was beginning to get defensive. He was sensing that Ernie Lambert had some terribly damaging information and his inexperience was leading him in the worst possible direction for a meeting of this nature.

"That's my question for you, Ernie. How do you expect me to believe this story? There is no way bonuses could be paid without mine or the board's knowledge. I need to know who your informant is and how creditable is this person? Because I'm afraid you've been led on a wild goose chase. Is this someone trying to cut a deal by delivering some bombshell story?"

By now, Ernie Lambert was really ticked off, but he was trying not to show his emotions. He laughed at the final part of Baxter's comment. "Sorry, Baxter, I wish that were true. Listen very closely because I'm about to end this meeting. I'm trying to do you favor. If the State Auditor shows up in the next few weeks and finds massive financial wrongdoing, you are gone, but if you are able to self report whatever has taken place, you aren't going to look quite so incompetent. Sleep on it and let me know what your decision is going to be."

"Uh, let me talk to my board president. What are you planning to do?"

"I have three options. If you take the steps to address the problem I will wait and let the Auditors office conduct the audit and then file charges based upon their results. Or I can convene a Grand Jury next week and start calling witnesses. This will be really messy for all parties."

"Ok, you said there were three."

"You don't want to know about the third option. It's the worst possible choice for you and the school. I promise you, I won't go that route unless you continue to act like an arrogant, tone deaf, ass hole." With that Ernie Lambert stood and thanked Baxter Flynn for coming. Flynn left without shaking Lambert's hand or making eye contact.

Ernie Lambert was a long-time friend to Craig Sizemore, board president of the Bouvier School Board. He would know within the next 12 hours if Baxter Flynn had decided to take a pro-active approach to his looming problem.

Bre Pattone arrived home two hours earlier than normal. Instead of meeting with Bre and addressing the serious allegations, Baxter Flynn took the easy way out in order to buy himself some time. He had the school's IT person lock Bre's computer log-in capability. Within 15 minutes after concluding his excruciating meeting with Ernie Lambert, Baxter Flynn had successfully removed Bre Pattone from any possible access to the Bouvier School District's computer system. When Bre complained to the school's IT guy about her inability to log-in, she was told they couldn't figure out what was wrong and that it might be early tomorrow morning before they could get her situation fixed. Bre tried to get Baxter Flynn to intervene on her behalf, but Baxter's secretary informed Bre in a rather curt manner that Baxter was meeting with the School Board President and was not to be disturbed.

Bre's arrival time wasn't expected by Rocko Gorski or the young girl he had become affectionate with over the past few weeks. As soon as Bre walked into the kitchen area of her home she heard loud screams, which sounded like a woman. She immediately ran upstairs to find Rocko and his new babe, a shapely but hard looking teenager named Jade Zeran, completely naked in her bed in quite the moment of affection.

The next few moments were picked up electronically by Mac Z. LeGarge and his MZL team. Hearing the screams and threats made Mac think he was back doing CIA detail in the Middle East. Then he heard the shots and the screams. Then there were two more shots and then the screams went silent. The next sound that he could hear was that of a female voice crying.

"Oh my God!!! What have I done? What have I done? What am I going to do? Where's the gun?" What did I do with the freaking gun?"

Mac Z. LeGarge couldn't believe his ears. It sounded like Bre Pattone was the last person standing. He and his team were under the assumption that Bre had blown away Rocko and his teenage babe, Jade, in a jealous rage and now she couldn't find the gun.

"Where did I lay the freaking gun? Ok, ok, thank God. I need to place it in his left hand."

The MZL team hadn't called 911 yet. They were wanting to get as much incriminating information on tape as possible before placing the call and Bre was giving them a treasure trove of stuff to hand over to Ernie Lambert when the time was right.

"Where did the bastard put the bank passcodes? He moved them. OMG, I've got to have them. I can't believe the cheating bastard moved the passcode book. Where are they? Where the hell are they? Dammit Rocko, where's the passcode book?"

There was silence after each question asked by Bre. This led Mac and his team to conclude that everyone in the home, except Bre, was dead. They also concluded that Bre was desperately trying to find the codes to the bank account where they housed most of the stolen school money. She seemed to be more concerned with getting access to the rogue bank account than disposing of or strategic placement the bodies. Mac Z. LeGarge wanted her away from the bank account as long as possible. So they decided that the time was right for the 911 call.

Posing as a neighbor walking their dog, a member of the MZL team placed the 911 call to the Barry County 911 Center. The context of the call was the sound of gun shots coming from Bre Pattone's address, 1411 Mill Creek Road in Bouvier. The 911 dispatcher informed the caller that an officer would be routed to the address immediately. Within 114 seconds the MZL team could hear a police siren from their mics at Bre's home. Mac Z. LeGarge wasn't concerned about the possibility of his bugging devices being found by the Bouvier Police Department. His equipment had previously escaped detection by Al-Qaeda terrorists, so he was confident that the Bouvier Police force wouldn't discover the devices. Mack and his team chuckled when they heard Bre yell, "Oh my God!" as she heard the police cars pull up in her drive way. It was now time for Bre Pattone to put on the best acting job of her life, because her life as a free person was on the line.

By the time Buford Blakeley arrived at the home of Bre Pattone the story being relayed to him and other members of the investigative team was that Bre Pattone killed Rocko Gorski and Jade Zeran in self-defense. She had arrived home earlier than usual to find Rocko and Jade in the process of stealing her jewelry and other valuables. When confronted, Rocko pulled his weapon and things went to hell from there. Buford couldn't contain his laughter when Bre repeated the story in his presence.

"You've got to be kidding me. They are buck naked and you're claiming self defense?"

Bre wasn't used to men having this type of attitude toward her. She huffed at Buford and then did a fake cry. "Rocko had the weapon when I walked into the room."

Buford loved that line. He started laughing uncontrollably, "Yeah, it sure looks like he had a weapon alright. So that's what you called his Johnson?" You called it a weapon? Damn girl, that thing must have been impressive."

As he listened to the exchange between Bre Pattone and Sheriff Buford Blakeley, Mac LeGarge couldn't contain his enjoyment. "I've never met Sheriff Blakeley, but I already love the guy." The rest of the MZL team shared their enjoyment of Buford Blakeley's professional approach. One person who wasn't particularly enjoying Buford's manner was Bre Pattone. When she heard Buford's line about Rocko's weapon she lost control and tried to slap him, but Buford caught Bre's hand before it could strike his fat cheek. Buford stood up and got right in Bre's face, "Listen Sugarbritches, your little game is over. In addition to murder, I'm going to have my good friend, Ernie Lambert add assaulting a police officer to what is going to be a laundry list of charges for you. Have you met Ernie Lambert? He happens to be the prosecuting attorney in Barry County. He will be the one who sends your sweet ass and big tits to death row."

Bre was in uncommon territory. She didn't have a man swooning over her and she didn't know how to react. She normally could use her body and looks to gain an advantage in tough situations, but Buford Blakeley wasn't interested, in fact he was mocking her.

"Go to hell, you fat bastard. I didn't murder anyone. You are the first person I'm going to sue for slander. I want my attorney and I want him now."

Buford was loving the confrontation with Bre, even if she had called him a fat bastard. He smiled, "Boys, let Sugarbritches have her cell phone to call her attorney. So who are you going to call, Sugarbritches?"

Bre snarled at Buford. It's Ms. Pattone for your information. I am calling Raleigh J. Calhoun. He will have me out of here within the next 30 minutes and then he will be suing you and the county for unlawful imprisonment, defamation, and who knows what else he can think of.

Buford Blakeley was laughing uncontrollably. His face was red from the laughter. "Don't waste your time on Raleigh. He would take an Islamic terrorist on as a client before he would take someone like you."

Bre was stung, but was trying not to show it. "Shut up, you fat jerk. What do you mean someone like me?"

"You don't want me to get started on that topic. There's not enough time in the day to describe you. I can assure you, Charlyn Belle Calhoun would divorce Raleigh J. Calhoun if he were to represent the town whore in a murder trial." This sent Bre into orbit. She tried to slap Buford again, but was stopped by one of his deputies. The screaming and obscenities coming from Bre were at a fever pitch when Ernie Lambert walked into the room.

This first thing Ernie saw was a great big smile on Buford Blakeley's fat face. He hadn't seen Buford this happy in a long, long time. Ernie had just entered the room and was already sick of hearing Bre's act. He motioned for Buford to join him in another room.

Once they had some privacy Ernie asked for a rundown on what Buford had learned from his review of the crime scene and Bre's statements. Buford relayed the position of the bodies and their clothing situation - or lack thereof. Buford wasn't buying Bre's story of self-defense. It didn't seem realistic with the positions of the naked bodies. He was confident that Bre's hand would test positive for gun residue. Plus, he believed that she had placed the gun in Rocko's hand after the shooting and that Rocko's hand will not test positive for gun residue – but her's would.

Ernie and Buford made the decision to hold off on filing murder charges until they had the test results back from the crime lab. The house would be closed off as a crime scene and Bre Pattone would be under 24 hour surveillance. Ernie liked this idea, plus he knew Judge Altus T. Claibourn was very particular about his preference in having all the primary evidence in place when it was a murder case, especially one as high profile as this one would be. Ernie also thought that having access to Bre's home might prove to be beneficial to the potential embezzlement case involving the Bouvier School District.

"Buford, I bet we will find evidence here linking her and that Rocko dude to Gordy's claim that she was stealing large amounts of money from the school."

Mac Z. LeGarge and his MZL team had a bug in the room being used by Ernie Lambert and Buford Blakeley. When LeGarge heard Ernie Lambert's comment he went ballistic. He had his team play back the recording of the conversation to make sure he had heard Lambert's words correctly. Upon confirmation, Mac Z. LeGarge knew he had to make several moves quickly to preserve their plan.

Chapter 13

Durwood Hardy was accustomed to being the person dispensing advice in some of the toughest situations in a person's life. Now he was the one needing advice in what was a bizarre situation, one that he was certain no other pastor had ever faced. Durwood Hardy was preparing to conduct the funeral for a person he was 99.99% confident was still alive. After his mind boggling meeting with Emerald Patrick, Durwood was trying to come to terms with what his responsibility was in this predicament. Should he conduct the service and act like he knew nothing about the possibility of Gordy Blanchard being alive and well? Or should he try to gracefully bow out of the service and hopefully do so in a manner that doesn't create suspicion and further controversy. After a fitful night of little, if any sleep, Durwood decided he should reach out to the one person that he could totally trust.

Durwood and Veronica Hardy had become close friends with Raleigh J. and Charlyn Belle Calhoun. The Calhoun's accepted the controversial marriage of Durwood and Veronica Hardy when many in Bouvier were less than accepting. The Calhoun's openness and understanding led the way for many others in Bouvier to follow suit and that in turn paved the way for Durwood and Veronica Hardy to remain in the Bouvier Lutheran Church.

After a phone conversation in which Raleigh could sense that something was really bothering Durwood, Raleigh J. Calhoun asked Durwood and Veronica to join he and Charlyn Belle for dinner. When the Hardy's arrived at the stately southern colonial home, located at the south end of Bouvier on five manicured acres, they were warmly greeted by Raleigh and Charlyn Belle. Charlyn Belle with her beautiful long black hair was in her late fifties but could easily pass for being in her 30s. That evening she was dressed in jeans and a black silk blouse, which gracefully accented her attractive figure. Raleigh was in his normal khakis and white dress shirt.

The first order of business was drinks. Charlyn Belle was known in her circle of friends for her killer Margarita recipe. Even if he was a pastor, Charlyn Belle knew Durwood Hardy could never pass up one of her legendary drinks with extra salt. Durwood and Veronica loved coming over to the Calhoun's for an occasional dinner. The atmosphere was always so warm, relaxed, and fun.

The dinner was an incredible ensemble of grilled pecan chicken, green beans mixed with grilled mushrooms, and baby baker potatoes. The finishing touch was Charlyn Belle's killer chocolate sheet cake topped with vanilla ice cream. Durwood and Veronica couldn't contain their praise for the dinner. Raleigh jokingly said he had worked all afternoon on the feast. Charlyn Belle loved that line and added, "Raleigh did stop to get the ice cream on his way home from the office."

Despite his desire not to talk about the topic and two feeble attempts to move the conversation elsewhere, the topic at dinner was the double murder at Bre Pattone's home. None of the four could ever remember such a tragic week in the history of Bouvier. First, it was the explosion that killed Gordy Blanchard and now the double murder at the home of the town whore, who happened to be the school's bookkeeper. Veronica and Charlyn Belle had no doubt that Bre had committed the murder after finding her lover boy in bed with a shapely teenage tramp. Charlyn Belle laughed, "I guess Bre got a dose of her own medicine and couldn't take it." Veronica agreed with Charlyn Belle's assessment of what had most likely gone down at Bre's home earlier in the day. Raleigh and Durwood were remarkably silent during the whole double murder discussion. So much so that their wives took notice.

Once dinner was concluded, Veronica, who looked stunning as usual while dressed in her elegant but casual manner, helped Charlyn Belle put the dishes away while Raleigh invited Durwood to his study, which was just off from the family's great room. Raleigh's study was furnished with a large leather sofa and two plush leather chairs. It also boasted a collection of great works of fiction, a favorite of Raleigh's. Charlyn Belle had tastefully decorated his home office in a manner that was both warm and intimidating.

Raleigh closed the door to his study. He could tell from his prior phone conversation that Durwood was stressed and needed to talk. Raleigh filled each of their cups with his favorite hazelnut coffee and asked Durwood how his week was going.

"Raleigh, I really appreciate the opportunity to talk in private. I am facing the most bizarre situation of my career and I know that says a lot considering what I've been through. I am presiding over Gordy's funeral on Sunday, but I'm not sure I can do the service. I'm afraid I will violate many codes of conduct by doing Gordy's service."

Raleigh wasn't expecting this. "Why would conducting Gordy's service violate your church's code of conduct?"

Durwood decided not to waste any time. He immediately blurted out, "Gordy's not dead!"

It took a lot to shake up Raleigh J. Calhoun, but what Durwood Hardy had just uttered had absolutely stunned him. "Did I hear you right, Durwood? Did you just say Gordy's not dead?"

"Yes, you heard right Raleigh."

If it had been anyone else, Raleigh would have been ready to call Judge Altus T. Claibourn to set up an emergency competency hearing, but

Raleigh could tell that Durwood knew some important facts that no one else knew or should know, and he had tremendous respect for Durwood.

"Durwood, am I safe to presume that you have learned this in your position as a pastor and in a confidential pastor-parishioner dialogue?"

"Yes, you are exactly right, Raleigh."

"Now, how or why do you know that Gordy is alive?"

At this point Durwood Hardy recited for Raleigh his meeting with Emerald Patrick, including the part where she answered the question of whether she had committed a crime or was a part of a conspiracy to commit a crime. Over the years, Raleigh J. Calhoun liked to joke with friends and colleagues that he had seen it all in his long legal career in Bouvier, but what he heard on this evening topped everything he had previously seen or experienced.

For a man who prided himself in being able to ask questions in almost any circumstance in order to obtain clarity, Raleigh was spellbound by Durwood's tale. For several moments, he didn't know what to say or ask. Durwood broke the silence by asking the question that had been driving him crazy for the past day, should he still perform Gordy's funeral?

Raleigh paused for a while before starting to answer Durwood's question. He squinted and rubbed his chin as he began to talk. "Durwood, I think we both know this comes down to doing what's right. Of course, that can be a slippery slide. What's right to you may not seem right to someone else. So let me ask you this. Who has hired you to perform the service?"

"I've been asked to preside over the service by Gordy's wife and parents."

"I presume they do not have the information you just shared with me?"

"I have not shared that information with them. Nor will I, unless I have to do so."

"Exactly, you cannot divulge this information unless you are ordered by a court of law to release it. It's privileged communication between a pastor and parishioner. So what will happen if you choose not to perform the funeral service at such a late notice? Will there be questions asked, etc?"

"Yes, there would be lots of questions and I would have to lie to preserve what I know."

"Exactly, and would that be right? Would it be right for you to have to lie? Would it be right for the Blanchard's to have to scramble at the last moment to find a pastor for their husband's and son's service? Would it be right to put them under any additional stress after what they've been through this week?"

Durwood smiled and answered, "No, it wouldn't be right, but what should I do with this information?"

Raleigh paused, "I know it sounds harsh, but you should do nothing unless you are required by a court decree to produce what you know."

"Shouldn't the Blanchard's have the opportunity to know that Gordy is still alive?"

"Great question, Durwood. That's a decision Gordy has to make and deal with, not you. He made the decision to flee and he is the one who has to deal with the consequences of that action, not you. However, I suspect the reasons for his decision will come out soon. Whether anyone ever finds out that Gord is still alive, who knows? But knowing Gordy, God love him, he will screw up some day and people will find out that he's living in Brazil or Belize or wherever people now go to get lost these days."

That brought a moment of levity, which was greatly needed. Durwood smiled, "You're right Raleigh, I love Gordy, but I just don't see him lasting on the lark. I foresee the day when someone on a Caribbean Cruise posts the headline: We just ran into Gordy Blanchard. He's alive in St. Thomas and is a golf pro at the Bermuda Triangle Diamond Course."

"Raleigh, I keep going back to the thought that I am committing a fraud by conducting a funeral for someone that I'm confident is still alive."

"Durwood, do you ask to see the body of the deceased for every funeral service that you conduct?"

"No, I don't."

"Are you confident that every funeral service you've conducted has been for someone really deceased?"

Durwood grinned, "I had never doubted it, until yesterday afternoon. Now I'm racking my brain wondering if this has ever happened before."

"Exactly, Durwood, you are performing a service at the request of the family. Proving or disproving death isn't your your job. That belongs to the County Coroner. I know it's scary considering our current Coroner is a Veterinarian, but that's how our Democracy works. The Blanchard's have asked you to lead the celebration of Gordy's life. Am I correct, Durwood?"

"So I am safe in holding to my oath of confidentiality between a Pastor and Parishioner?"

"Durwood, you handled your meeting with Emerald perfectly. Before she told you the details of finding Gordy, you specifically asked her if she had committed a crime or was part of a conspiracy to commit a crime. The answer was clearly, no. Emerald was in the right place at the right time and was nosy enough to find out what the heck had happened. She did nothing wrong. She had not committed a crime. So you have to maintain that confidentiality. Otherwise, your career as a trusted Pastor is over and it should be. I would never come to you for counseling, nor would anyone else, if you were to break this confidence."

Raleigh had come down pretty hard, but he knew he had to make his point. Durwood wasn't offended by Raleigh's candor. To the contrary, he appreciated Raleigh's expertise and the way in which he dispensed advice. He was never condescending, unlike many of the other attorneys Durwood had encountered. Raleigh was very down to earth, matter of fact, and most of the time, very graceful in the way he broke down the situations presented to him. His vote of confidence was exactly what Durwood needed in the midst of such a complex and bizarre situation. He thanked Raleigh for taking the time to listen to his problem and providing his expert advice.

As they were leaving the Calhoun's beautiful colonial home on a near perfect September evening, Veronica Hardy saw a noticeable difference in her husband's composure. A quiet calm or confidence was back with Durwood. Once they arrived home, Durwood slept the best he had since the presumed death of Gordy Blanchard.

Chapter 14

The next morning Buford Blakeley arrived at Ruby's Pancakes and More to find two faces that he hadn't seen in a few days - Emerald Patrick and disgraced Bouvier Fire Chief, Leroy Boulevard. Emerald's face was a pleasant surprise for Buford, while seeing Leroy's mug wasn't really what Buford was hoping to see at 7 am. Not only was Leroy at Ruby's, he had the nerve to be sitting in Buford's normal spot at the Board of Director's table.

Things got ugly fast. Buford wanted his normal seat, "Leroy, why don't you haul your fat ass to the end of the table."

Leroy hurled a couple of obscenities toward Buford, which essentially summarized his belief that he would sit anywhere he damn well pleased. Buford stood over Leroy, "You know Leroy, for a guy who made an ass of himself on TV a few days ago, you're acting pretty smug right now. Why don't you go crawl back under that rock where you've been hiding and crying since your stellar TV debut."

Leroy laughed, "I was right about what I said, and I want an apology. I want it right here in front of all your friends."

Buford stood and looked at Leroy like he was an idiot, "An apology, an apology for what? If anyone needs to apologize it's you. You need to apologize for embarrassing Bouvier on TV."

"Screw you, Barney Fife. I was right. The explosion was intentional. That bimbo with the big tits also murdered Gordy."

Sitting in his favorite seat at Ruby's was one thing, but being called Barney Fife was the unforgivable sin as far as Buford Blakeley was concerned. Buford hauled his big right hand back and was ready to pop Leroy Boulevard on the jaw when he was stopped by Dr. Galen Penn, Bouvier's primary Veterinarian and the County Coroner of Barry

County. When Buford turned to see who had captured his hand he was furious. His distain for Dr. Penn was a longstanding fact for many familiar with politics in Bouvier and Barry County. Buford yelled out, "Doc, get the hell away from here and go back to killing dogs, which is apparently your specialty." Years earlier, Doc Penn had used too much anesthesia when he operated on Buford's beloved German Shepherd, Ralphie. Poor ole Ralphie never woke up from the surgery and Buford had never gotten over it.

Emerald was in the back of the cafe when she heard a terrible commotion. She ran out to find a scene that included Doc Penn trying to choke Buford Blakeley. To survive, Buford was trying to stab Penn and Boulevard with a butter knife as he was lying flat on his back being held down by Leroy Boulevard. Emerald immediately picked up a chair and popped Doc Penn across the head, which sent him flying off Buford Blakeley. Leroy Boulevard looked up at Emerald with a frightened expression and she said, "Leroy get off Buford or you're next."

As the parties began to separate Emerald began to set everyone straight. Holding her chair as a reminder of what she was capable of doing, Emerald gave Buford, Doc, and Leroy their instructions, "Ok, here's the deal, all of you are going to clean up this mess. Then you're going to go home and get your clothes and manners cleaned up. If you do that then you're welcome for lunch. Otherwise, don't bother coming back if you're going to act like a bunch of two year olds. And this better not resume in the parking lot because I have a group of ladies from the Methodist Church coming for breakfast and they are not going to be subjected to a honkey tonk atmosphere on my property. Are we clear?"

All three nodded in embarrassment. Before they headed out the door, Buford yelled back, "Em, what's the lunch special going to be?"

"Buford, it's going to be fried chicken, mashed potatoes, with green beans, and chocolate sheet cake for desert. Don't be late!'

Within five minutes a video of the last moments of the morning fight at Ruby's had made its way to Facebook. It was an instant classic. Within the next hour the video was loaded on YouTube. By 8:30 am the regional TV stations were airing the video with the caption, 'Bouvier Fire Chief, Leroy Boulevard, is back in action.'

Shortly after the morning breakfast debacle at Ruby's, Buford Blakeley received a cell phone call from Ernie Lambert as he was going through the drive-thru lane at the Bouvier McDonalds. Having to eat a McDonald's breakfast after having his heart set on some of Ruby's biscuits and gravy had put Buford in a really bad mood. Ernie could immediately tell something was wrong as soon as Buford answered.

"Damn, Buford, you sound even surlier than normal. What's your problem, Ruby's run out of biscuits and gravy this morning?"

"Thanks a lot! So I guess you heard what happened?"

Ernie immediately knew there was trouble. "Uh, Buford, no I haven't heard anything. I was calling to tell you that I need you in my office in 30 minutes. So what's wrong?"

"Oh hell, I don't have time to get into it now. By the time you get to the office, I'm sure the gossip hounds at the courthouse will be giving their account of what went down at Ruby's"

"Hold on there, Joe Friday, quickly tell me what the hell has happened."

"Well, my morning started with breakfast in the company of Doc Penn and Leroy Boulevard and ended with Doc and Leroy trying to choke me to death while I tried to stab them with a butter knife. Emerald broke things up by beating the hell out of Doc with a chair, but she invited us all back for lunch. So how the hell is your morning so far?"

Ernie burst out laughing, "It's going a helluva lot better than yours. Get your ass in my office in 30 minutes and try not to get into a fight between now and then. It's important, and don't be late or grumpy."

"Bastard! I'll be right over."

By the time Buford Blakeley arrived at the Barry County Courthouse, the TV in the lobby was on one of the TV stations in Springfield. The station was showing a replay of the fight at Ruby's. A group of courthouse workers were standing around watching the replay. A very mad and embarrassed Buford Blakeley ran upstairs as fast as his 328 pound body could move. As soon as he walked into the waiting room at Ernie Lambert's office, Buford realized that Ernie's staff had been watching a replay of the Ruby's brawl. He was in no mood to be joked with, but that wasn't going to stop Ernie's mischievous staff. After about the third insult, Ernie came out of his office and saved everyone from having to watch Buford totally blow a gasket and unleash a massive bombardment of obscenities.

Once they were inside Ernie's office, Ernie tried to get Buford calmed down. "Listen, you've got to let this go. If you get mad and make a big deal of it, it will become an even bigger deal. Suck it up, grin, and act like you don't give a rip."

"Easy for you to say. You're not the one on TV being laughed at and ridiculed."

"True, but we've got too many important matters to tend to for you to be whining around about your plight in life."

After several moments of silence, Ernie realized that even if he was still really mad and hurt, Buford was now able to focus on what he had to say.

"So what's so damn important?"

"I've been contacted by a gentleman named Mac Z. LeGarge. Have you ever heard of him?"

"Sounds familiar."

"LeGarge is a retired military big wig and now runs an upscale security firm. The U.S. Attorney out of Tallahassee, Florida called late yesterday and asked if we would meet with LeGarge."

"U.S. Attorney in Tallahassee, Florida? Why the hell would they be calling you?"

"I was wondering the same thing, until she said it pertained to financial fraud at the Bouvier School District and the death of Gordy Blanchard."

"You've got to be kidding me. Why would the U.S. Attorney in Tallahassee, Florida be interested in what's going on in Bouvier, Missouri?"

"I asked the same thing. All she would say was that Mr. LeGarge would clear all this up for us."

"When is he coming to see us?"

"In about 15 minutes."

"Oh hell, thanks a lot for the advance notice."

"I tried to call earlier, but you were too busy trying to kill Doc and Leroy with a butter knife while they were kicking your ass."

Buford started to storm out of the room before Ernie got him calmed down. "You've got to tell me the story when you're in a better mood."

"That's never gonna happen."

While Buford and Ernie were waiting for the arrival of Mac

Z. LeGarge, Ernie received a phone call from an irate Rex Moffitt. Rex had represented Bre Pattone in one of her divorces and was now advising her after the shooting deaths at her home. As usual, Rex was long on threats and short on actual case law as it pertained to his client. He was demanding the immediate curtailment of the 24 hour surveillance of Bre. He spouted several amendments of the constitution that were being violated by the unfair and arbitrary gestapo type tactics being used by the Barry County Sheriff's Department. After he finished his tirade, Ernie calmly said, "Rex, for your information, the 13th amendment to the U.S. Constitution abolished slavery in the United States; please tell me how that applies in this situation."

Rex wasn't pleased with Ernie's reply, "What the hell are you talking about?"

"Well, Rex, you cited the 13th amendment as one of the violations of the law that we had committed and I just can't see how that applies. How about you go back to your office and do a little refresher on the various constitutional amendments and we'll talk later when you are better prepared." As Ernie hung up the phone, he could hear Rex Moffitt yelling a multitude of obscenities. Ernie smiled as he was confident that when he ran into Rex later in the day that Rex will be cordial and act like nothing bad had happened. Such was the life of dealing with the bipolar Rex Moffitt.

Once his phone call with Rex Moffitt concluded, Ernie's secretary notified him that a Mac Z. LeGarge was waiting to see him.

Chapter 15

Mac Z. LeGarge had to call in more favors than he really wanted to in his preparation for his meeting with the Barry County Prosecuting Attorney, Ernie Lambert, and Barry County Sheriff, Buford Blakeley. The 'intelligence' that he had gathered over the previous weeks was illegal and no credible judge in the United States would allow it into a court of law. Mac's challenge was to get all of his recordings validated by a legal authority. Through his previous work at the Pentagon and at the highest levels of the intelligence field, Mac Z. LeGarge had developed a vast collection of friends and contacts who came in handy in situations just like this one. This time the Assistant Attorney General of the United States, R. Dalton Brownsworth, came to the rescue for Mac.

In his previous life, Mac had been instrumental in assisting Brownsworth in his quest to track down a key informant for the prosecution of a ringleader in the Mexican meth cartel. Mac had gone to unbelievable measures, which R. Dalton Brownsworth did not want to even remotely know about in his successful detainment of the informant. Thanks to Mac's work, Brownsworth successfully prosecuted the Mexican drug lord, and for that Brownsworth always tried to help out Mac Z. LeGarge anytime he could. In turn, Mac tried not to burden Brownsworth with requests unless he felt as if they were very important. Because of Mac's relationship with Blair Jennings, he knew this was one time he would call R. Dalton Brownsworth, if all else failed.

R. Dalton Brownsworth had commanded his Tallahassee office to prepare a summary memo, which provided some plausible basics as to why they had become interested in Rocko Gorsko. This would be the memo that Mac Z. LeGarge would soon hand off to Ernie Lambert.

The summary memo covered the basics of the investigation in the following manner: A money manager in the Florida Gulf Coast area had become privy to a client's money movements that appeared to be very suspicious. Following her required due diligence, the money manager filed a Suspicious Activity Report, also known as a SAR, regarding the client's activities. The SAR filing made its way to the FBI office in Tallahassee, which handled it in coordination with the U.S. Attorney's office there. The U.S. Attorney's office retained a security firm, MZL & Associates, to assist in the electronic data collection of their investigation. In the midst of their investigation of Rocko Gorski's alleged money laundering the MZL team discovered a potential murder conspiracy and multi million dollar embezzlement in Bouvier, Missouri.

Mac Z. LeGarge was welcomed into Ernie Lambert's office. Dressed in a blue blazer, grey slacks, a white shirt, Mac looked very impressive but not overdressed or too slick. He was slightly overweight and had short grey hair. Ernie introduced Buford Blakeley to Mac. Mac warmly thanked both of them for taking the time to meet with him on such short notice. Ernie asked Mac if he wanted coffee, tea, water, or a soft drink. Mac smiled and replied, "Is it too early for some bourbon?" Ernie and Buford immediately liked Mac and his easy going manner. He was nothing like Ernie had expected.

Ernie laughed, "It is for me, but after the way Buford's day started he may be ready to join you."

Mac smiled, "Sheriff, hang in there, I've had much worse starts in my day, but I have to admit, I really liked the spunk of the young lady who owns the cafe."

Buford finally chimed in, "So Mac, you saw the video, as well?"

"Sheriff, I did, but don't worry, I've seen much worse. Those guys must be really stupid or total ass holes."

Buford Blakeley was now in love with Mac Z. LeGarge.

Mac decided to dive right in and discuss why he had requested the meeting on such short notice. He began his presentation in a calm manner that was made even easier by his deep southern accent and slow cadence that came with his life as a true southerner and a career of providing briefings for people such as General Norman Schwarzkopf and at least three U.S. Presidents. In addition, he provided Ernie and Buford a copy of his resume for reference and to provide credibility. Ernie had already Googled him and was thoroughly impressed before Mac even walked into his office.

After his intro, Mac handed Ernie and Buford copies of the summary memo that he had prepared for the U.S. Attorney's office in Tallahassee. He gave them several minutes to read the summary. Mac enjoyed watching their expressions as they read about the money laundering, murder conspiracy, and multi million-dollar embezzlement. Both appeared to be stunned for several moments.

Mac broke the silence, "And we have saved all of the electronic recordings from the home of Bre Pattone, which I am authorized to turn over to you, assuming you want to take the case."

Ernie did a double take, "You have electronic recordings from Bre's home?"

Mac smiled before he replied. "Yes, Ernie, in fact at this moment we are still monitoring her home."

"How long do the recordings go back and how is the quality?"

"We were able to penetrate her home prior to the death of Milford Blanchard, Jr. You will be glad to know that the quality of the surveillance is excellent. To streamline this meeting, we have everything a prosecutor could ever want. We have Bre Pattone and her deceased boyfriend discussing their plan to kill Gordy Blanchard as a way to hide their embezzlement of millions of dollars from the Bouvier School District. Plus, we captured the murder of Rocko Gorski and Jade Zeran by Bre. Understand, I cannot hand it over until I have total assurance that your Judge Claiborne will accept it without bringing in the U.S. Attorneys office in Tallahassee. They view this as your case and they have much bigger fish to fry down in Florida. Getting called up to Southwest Missouri isn't their cup of tea. They see the chances of getting a conviction being much greater with you and your expertise prosecuting a local murder and embezzlement case than they would have with a group of jurors in Northwest Florida."

Once they had absorbed the most fascinating 45 minutes of their careers, Ernie called Judge Altus T. Claiborne's office for an emergency conference. The judge's secretary wasn't pleased with the request, but after a few moments she said the judge would see them in 30 minutes.

Judge Altus T. Claibourn was in his early seventies. He stood five feet eleven inches tall and weighed about one hundred and seventy five pounds. A trim and very handsome man, he grew his gray hair somewhat long and combed it straight back. Altus Claibourn gave the appearance of an eccentric college professor, but he still possessed one of the keenest legal minds of the circuit judges in the state of Missouri. He had originally planned to retire when he reached the age of sixty, but those plans went out the window because his wife was one of the counties biggest spenders and he knew that retirement was a recipe for bankruptcy. In truth, the real reason was that he loved the job too much

The esteemed judge welcomed the group into his plush study, which was located in the northeast corner of the Barry County Justice

Center. When the center was constructed, Judge Claibourn insisted on having large windows that would allow the morning sun into his office. Plus, he loved the second floor view of Bouvier. Claibourn didn't care about the afternoon sun from the west as he rarely worked late in the day. It was one of the perks of being the senior judge in his circuit.

Judge Claibourn was in a surprisingly good mood when they arrived at his office, and they soon found out why. Judge Claibourn motioned for everyone to sit down before he began his opening salvos.

"Well gentlemen it is a pleasure to see you this morning. And it is an indeed pleasure to meet you Mr. LeGarge. I sincerely appreciate your service to our country. Thanks to you and your service, the world is a safer place and there are fewer drug lords and crazy bastards wanting to blow up America. That's not the only thing I appreciate. I have been a circuit judge for a long, damn time and until today the Office of the Attorney General of the United States has never seen the need to call ole Altus T. Clairbourn. Thanks to Mr. LeGarge, I had a very nice conversation with our Assistant Attorney General of the United States over the criminal division of the Department of Justice, Mr. R. Dalton Brownsworth. He seems to be a very nice and proper gentleman. He speaks very highly of you, Mr. LeGarge. Before we start, who would like something to drink?"

Everyone declined until they saw Judge Claibourn pull out his favorite bottle of Kentucky bourbon. "I know it's early, but I think we all need a good stiff drink." Everyone smiled and no one declined the Judge's offer. Buford Blakeley was thinking about how horrible his day had started and now he's drinking bourbon with Judge Claibourn and some military big wig who is buds with the Attorney General of the United States. Talk about a turn in fate!

Judge Claibourn continued after everyone had been supplied with a proper helping of his finest bourbon.

"Mr. LeGarge, I can assure you that we have no desire or need of assistance from the U.S. Attorney or his office in Tallahassee. No disrespect for those fine folks, but Ernie, Buford, and I are quite capable for properly moving forward with the evidence you and the FBI in Florida have obtained. I don't want to hear any of the recordings until they are presented into the court record. Please be assured that I will have no problem in accepting the evidence that has been turned over to Mr. Lambert."

Mac Z. LeGarge had met a lot of interesting and intelligent people, as well as exceptional characters in his career, but Judge Altus T. Claibourn had to be one of the most intelligent, charismatic, entertaining, and eccentric people he had ever met. He immediately loved the guy and this guy was hidden in the Ozark's hills of Southwest Missouri.

LeGarge handed the summary memo to Judge Claibourn. They each sipped on their bourbon glasses as the Judge read the document. Ernie Lambert sensed he was starting to get a buzz just as the Judge finished his review of the memo. Once Claibourn was completed with his review, Mac Z. LeGarge communicated the extent of their electronic recordings. Judge Claibourn once again indicated his desire not to hear the specific recordings until they were presented in a pre-trial hearing.

Before he concluded the meeting, Judge Claibourn asked what the extent of the charges would be coming against Bre Patttone. "So, should I expect to see three murder charges, an act of terrorism through the bombing of a governmental building, along with the embezzlement charges?"

Mac immediately replied, "Your honor, I would envision two murder charges, conspiracy to commit murder, and embezzlement."

"Two murder charges, not three? And what about the explosion of the Blanchard Administration Building?"

"No your honor, based upon our recordings, they were planning to murder Mr. Blanchard, but he died before they could pull it off. Bre and Rocko had a huge argument and fight the morning of Blanchard's death. Bre angrily voiced her opinion that Rocko hadn't moved fast enough with their plan to kill Blanchard and complete the last wire transfer to move the school money. So, Sheriff Blakeley, your fat buddy, Mr. Boulevard is not correct. The recordings will prove that point."

"You're kidding. Poor ole Gordy never could catch a break. So how much money has been stolen from the school?"

"From what I have been told, it's over two million and could be more. They are looking at one other possible account being used by Rocko Gorski."

"Oh my God! Am I to understand that the money has been intercepted by the U.S. Attorney's office?"

"Yes! The school was very fortunate the money manager determined something wasn't right with Rocko's account. Otherwise, you would be looking at the closing of the Bouvier School District."

Ernie Lambert, Buford Blakeley, and Altus T. Claibourn sat stunned when they heard the conclusion of Mac Z. LeGarge's report.

Judge Claibourne concluded, "I don't know who to thank, but please extend our gratitude to whoever discovered what was going on here, otherwise we would be facing an unbelievable tragedy. The closing of the school and the impact on the students, hundreds of teachers and support staff losing their jobs, local bond holders losing millions of dollars, it would have been devastating, beyond comprehension. So Ernie and

Buford, do you have a good idea on what you need to do next?"

Ernie smiled. "Yes, your honor, we will proceed with the arrest of Bre Pattone within the hour. I will immediately be in contact with Baxter Flynn to provide him with a brief summary of the situation, so he can make arrangements to find a new bookkeeper - preferably one who isn't a manipulating bimbo. Buford and Mr. LeGarge will coordinate the collection of the electronic surveillance at Ms. Pattone's home. Your honor, I have to give you notice, that Bre has retained Rex Moffitt, so you will get to see Rex on a regular basis for the next few months."

This wasn't what Claibourn wanted to hear. "That guy is so incompetent. No telling what types of motions he will be filing."

Ernie laughed and retold the story from earlier that morning when Rex called and cited all of the various constitutional violations that were being committed in Bre's case, including the 13th Amendment.

Altus T. Claibourn loved the story. "He didn't really cite the 13th Amendment to the Constitution? My Lord, ole Rex is a total fool. How in the world did he get his law degree?"

With that, the meeting concluded as the men exchanged pleasantries. Mac Z. LeGarge was relieved beyond belief that the meetings with Ernie Lambert and Altus T. Claibourn went so well. He came away from the meeting with total admiration for all three men. Mac was also relieved that no one asked for details on the money manager who intercepted the money laundering operation. Blair Jennings would be thrilled to know that she never came up in the discussion.

As they were leaving, Buford caught Ernie and quietly reminded him not to allow his assistant prosecutor, Linsome Laimers, access to any part of the case.

"Just remember, Ernie, good ole Linsome is a backstabbing weasel who would love to have your job. We both know this case has taken a bunch of short cuts with our new best friend Mac's help. He's not above leaking stuff to make himself look good at your expense. When you get a free moment, you should fire his sorry ass."

"You don't have to worry. Linsome won't go near this case."

"I don't know about you, but I'm really looking forward to lunch, now, and I'm up for some more of that bourbon later this afternoon."

Ernie laughed and shook his head as they parted the Barry County Justice Center.

Chapter 16

Blair Jennings was thrilled to see Gordy Blanchard when he arrived at her stately beachfront home in Seaside, Florida. They hugged and headed into her kitchen area where she had some delicious muffins and other goodies waiting for Gordy. Blair didn't cook much, but she was friends with a gentleman who had just started a bakery in the Seaside area. Gordy had grabbed a burger for dinner at a fast food joint outside of Pensacola. All he had asked for in their earlier conversation was something sweet to eat when he arrived.

Blair could immediately tell that Gordy was exhausted both mentally and physically after this sixteen-hour drive from Bouvier. Gordy collapsed into one of the bar stools situated around the center bar area of Blair's expansive kitchen. He looked at Blair and said, "I can't thank you enough for everything you've done for me. I was in way over my head in so many ways and just totally screwed everything up." Gordy stopped as he began to tear up. He didn't want to cry, but his emotions were starting to pour forth for the first time in a long, long time.

"Gordy, it's ok. You did what you had to do. This Bre chick is evil. She has been manipulating her way through life and you just happened to be her next target. With you being gone, she will be caught and exposed for what she really is. I am totally confident that Mac's plan will work and probably work to perfection."

"So you have total confidence in Mac?"

"Yes. Absolutely! Do you have any concerns?"

"Did the Emerald thing really have to go the way it did? I mean, do you have any idea how horrible it was to see her in Mobile and to then just drive away? Did it really have to play out like that?"

"Gordy, I know it must have been terrible to drive away from

Emerald. How else could it have gone? Mac is a smart guy. Everything in this situation has played out exactly as he said it would. When he said Emerald was stalking you none of us believed it, but he was right. Emerald did precisely what he said she would do. Did you really think she would follow you after the explosion, all the way to Mobile, Alabama?"

"No! I didn't know she was following me. We had a script in case something happened and Emerald became suspicious, but Mac had left me in the dark that she was on my tail. I didn't know anything until he called me on the way to the Starbucks in Mobile. That's where he gave me my instructions. The poor girl had driven all the way to Mobile and I had to let her drive off?"

"Mac is a pro. Everything he has done has been for a reason. You're lucky, Gordy. Mac has never let anyone from someone's prior life know about their new life, until Emerald. I hope it doesn't backfire on you and me. No, let me rephrase it. It will not backfire on me. Do you really know the steps that have been taken, the laws that have broken in order to save your life and the future of the Bouvier School District? I haven't told you the full extent of Bre's embezzlement. The wires to Rocko's account, not including the bonuses paid to herself, would have permanently closed down the school. All jobs would have been lost. The local people who have purchased millions of dollars of school bonds would have lost all of their money. The school and Bouvier would have been devastated financially, and you would have been dead. So, Mac has been pretty busy trying to clean up this horrible mess, while trying to work out a future for you that will hopefully make you live happily."

Gordy sat with his head down. He had tears rolling down his cheeks. "I'm sorry. I'm sorry. I shouldn't have complained about

Mac. This is bizarre beyond comprehension, but please let me express how much I appreciate everything you and Mac have done. I am not ungrateful, at all. I'm still in a daze after walking away from my life and starting a new one fresh. It's still hard to comprehend despite the planning that went into this move. It's surreal."

Blair gave Gordy a hug. "Gord, it's going to be a rough few weeks making the transition. I totally understand, and I know you appreciate everything that has been done. I know you would do anything for me. You're my one true friend."

"I love you, Blair."

"I love you, too, Gordy."

"I'm sorry I made such a mess of things at the school."

"Ok, Gordy, one rule here. No self-pity. You are a wonderfully talented and smart person. Bre Pattone is one conniving bitch. She has worked her magic all of her life and if it hadn't been you, she would have targeted someone else. There is no need to apologize to me."

With tears in his eyes, Gordy quietly spoke, "Thank you, Blair."

Before he crashed from the exhaustion of the sixteen hour drive, not to mention, starting a total new life, Gordy talked with Blair about her life in Seaside. He thoroughly enjoyed hearing Blair talk about life on the beach and managing the money of some of America's wealthiest people. By 11:00 p.m. he was sound asleep snoring away in the beautiful guest bedroom in Blair's five-bedroom beach mansion.

Gordy Blanchard awakened to the beautiful sight and sounds of the Gulf of Mexico outside his bedroom window. He had his best night's sleep in months. His mind immediately went to Bouvier and what was happening there in the wake of his death. He could visualize the scene at

Ruby's with all of the members of the board of directors table providing their best insight on what had caused the worst explosion in the history of Bouvier. Before he could go through the progression of what his parents and wife were experiencing, Blair cracked open his door to see if he was still asleep.

"Well there's the sleepyhead. Did you sleep well?"

"Great! I could get used to sleeping to the sound of the ocean in the background. Seriously, I can't remember the last time I slept this well."

"I'm tickled. I could tell. When's the last time you slept past 9 am?"

"You're kidding me? It's nine o'clock?"

"No, it's actually almost ten o'clock."

"Oh my God. I feel like such a bum. I haven't slept late since maybe our college days after a drunken Friday night on Walnut Street."

"Gordy! I have no recollection of any such nights in college. Especially on Walnut Street in Springfield."

They had a good laugh. Gordy and Blair had the type of friendship in which they could immediately pick up from where they had left off, even if it had been months between conversations. Gordy had been to Blair's home three years earlier, but the moment he walked into her beautiful home on the previous night he felt right at home.

Gordy threw on some shorts, an old St. Louis Cardinals t-shirt, and joined Blair on her spacious deck, which overlooked the Gulf of Mexico. Blair had donuts, which Gordy admitted were the best he had ever eaten and that was saying a lot considering Gordy had mooched every donut available from every hospitality room in his career as a coach. The Donut Hole would soon be Gordy's new go to place for a breakfast on the go. It was a legendary bakery shop on the Gulf and Gordy was soon discovering why.

Gordy and Blair spent the day relaxing on the beach, which sat just a few feet from the bedroom that was his temporary home. The beautiful white sand felt incredible to Gordy as he made his way to the beach chairs Blair had lined up along the shore of the Gulf. It was a perfect day. The temperature reached a high of 84 degrees and there wasn't a cloud in the sky. Gordy thoroughly enjoyed being able to soak up the sun beside Blair who looked amazing in her two-piece red swimsuit. He thought Blair looked even better than she did in her prime as an All American volleyball player at Missouri State University. Gordy couldn't help but catch himself staring at Blair's stunning physique lying on the white sand. After all these years, Gordy was still in love with his first love - Blair Jennings.

Blair and Gordy spent the entire afternoon consuming Sam Adams Octoberfest Beer, baking in the sun, and swimming in the warm Gulf waters. Neither could remember the last time either had consumed that much beer. It had been the most enjoyable day Gordy had experienced in many years. Blair remarked that this was the most she had relaxed in a long, long time.

The next morning after breakfast, Blair drove Gordy down to the local marina in her white Audi sportster convertible. As he sat in the passenger seat with the breeze and sun splashing his face Gordy felt real for the first time in years. This was Blair's plan. She knew Gordy would never escape the worries about his parents and the guilt for being manipulated by Bre and fleeing Bouvier, but she knew that with the right culture and environment, Gordy could move forward and realize the potential she had witnessed as he grew up in Bouvier and while in college at Missouri State. Very few had truly seen the potential and the drive Blair sensed Gordy could realize. The next day was spent on Blair's large excursion boat as they took in the sights up and down the Emerald Coast between Destin and Panama City Beach. Blair's staff was shocked when she informed them that she would be taking two days off, but they were glad to see her finally take some time to relax and enjoy herself.

The day on Blair's boat was even more enjoyable than the previous day at the beach. They talked about everything from growing up in the Lutheran Church in Bouvier to their first days in elementary school to their college days at Missouri State.

With the sun basking down on the ocean waters, Gordy looked at Blair lying back in the lounger, while she sat there taking in the sun as it reflected perfectly off her stylish black Ray Ban shades, as her beautiful blond hair flowed with the gulf breeze. He marveled at her and what she had achieved.

"Blair, you've accomplished things beyond imagination, especially from what we said we hoped to do back in our nights of drinking ice cold Budweiser at Terrence Boggs Barbecue joint in college. Is there anything else you want to attain?"

Blair looked at Gordy for several moments before taking off her Ray Ban's. "Gord, you haven't forgotten have you? On those nights of drinking Budweiser and watching the Cardinals at Terrence Boggs joint you said you really didn't want to go into education but your dad would have disowned you if you had taken another path. What did you really want to do?"

"I wanted to work with athletes and help them with life outside of and beyond competition. I wanted to be more than just an agent, but to be a trusted advisor."

"Yes, exactly! And you would have been amazing at it. You were a great athlete. You knew what it took to be successful on the field of play, and you minored in Psychology. You were interested in and had education involving the mental side of the game and life beyond sports. That's what I want to accomplish. I want to see you excel at something you love doing. You've attained so much in education - becoming an assistant superintendent at such a young age, but you have repeatedly told me it wasn't what you wanted to do. I want to be a resource for wherever you choose to go. It might be sports management and mentoring, or being a golf pro, or the business opportunity you've discussed."

As he sat there wiping tears from his eyes, Gordy was still having a hard time figuring out why Blair would exhaust so much time, energy, resources, and professional reputation to help him hide and find a new life.

"Blair, you are amazing. Why me? You have done so much to save me and have put so much time, money, not to mention your professional reputation, to save me. Why?"

"You have always been there for me. It hasn't always been a bed of roses for me. Being gay is tough. I'm not trying to whine or ask for pity. I'm just stating the facts. There are still a lot of people who hate us, but way back in our college days, not only did they hate us, most couldn't even understand or comprehend a person being gay. Except you, Gordy Blanchard. The night you told me that you loved me and that you wanted to be more than best friends was incredible. It meant so much to know how you felt about me, and it meant even more to know how you felt about me when I told you I was gay. You have no idea how much confidence it gave me to know that my best friend would love me knowing that I was gay. That confidence propelled me to go out into the business world and to give it a try. I will never forget you agreeing to be my date when I went on my first big job interview. Do you remember that?"

Gordy laughed out loud. "How could I forget it? That guy we had dinner with was a total arrogant pant load?"

Blair couldn't help but laugh. "Yes, that was the human resources guy. He was the guy doing the hiring and he was such a big macho homophobe. You being my date sealed the deal for me, as he was suspicious of me since I was a tall unmarried female athlete. If I hadn't gotten that job, I don't know where I would have been in my career, but more importantly, you were there to support me any way possible. You flew all the way down to Orlando to do that dinner, and then you were there to help celebrate when I got the job. I've always known you would be there if I needed anything Gordy."

Gordy smiled and tried to hold back his tears. "That was an incredible night. We celebrated at that neat sports bar while the World Series was on TV. The one thing that stood out to me about that macho homophobe was I really think he was a closet homosexual."

"Why's that?"

"The theory I've developed over the years is that those who are over the top macho and are constantly trashing gays are usually trying to hide their homosexual tendencies for career or cultural purposes."

Blair smiled, "There is a lot of truth to that. In fact, that guy was later fired when it came out that he was sexually harassing some hot young man in the management trainee program. See that shows your true gift that would be great with mentoring and or coaching athletes."

After consuming a few more beers and soaking up the sun, Gordy had one more topic that was racking his brain.

"Blair, if I had stayed, was there any way I could have conceivably escaped going to prison or dying?"

Blair paused before she answered. "You know, that was a terribly hard decision to make. I told Mac that before he offered this path to take, we better be absolutely sure it is the right choice. To go down the path we took is extraordinary. The resources to plan it, not to mention the laws that have been broken and the favors extended by people in very high places make this a tremendous undertaking. If there had been a more plausible or better choice we would have recommended it, absolutely. We really broke it down into several pieces. Could you have survived the legal challenges of embezzlement, obstruction of public funds, etc? I sat down with a very good friend who teaches criminal law at the University of Florida. I never gave names, places or anything like that, but I gave him the basic framework of your situation. He reviewed it for a few days and came back with the recommendation that there was a 75% chance that you would be convicted and would spend a good portion of your adult life in prison."

Gordy sat on his side of the boat in silence. "Did he see any chance of us being able to pin it all on Bre?"

"He felt as if that chance was a big gamble. In a case like this sometimes it comes down to who has the best attorney. She had done everything right to pin the embezzlement on you, and you know her attorney would have played the sexual harassment card. The photos of you with your hands on her large breasts would have been damning. The only way to get the evidence from the wire taps of her home presented publicly, where she and Rocko discuss the embezzlement and the plan to kill you, was to have you gone. Plain and simple. The wire taps were illegal. Mac has had to pull in a large number of favors from people in very high places to make recordings at Bre's home legitimate. The next piece to review was; what was going to hurt your parents the worst? Was it you being disgraced and going to prison while the school went under financially, or you dying?"

Gordy paused for a moment before he could reply. "And I chose dying. I didn't want to see my parents go through the ordeal of the trial and the school going bankrupt. Plus, my parents would have expended a big chuck of their retirement to try to save my ass with no assurance that the legal defense would be successful."

"Exactly, Gordy and the next question was; could we have kept you alive, if you had chosen to stay? Based upon Mac's assessment, the answer to that was; 'no!' Rocko would have found a way to kill you. Unfortunately Gordy, either way your parents were going to have a funeral for you. This way, on Sunday your life will be celebrated. They will be heartbroken, but proud parents. The heartbreak will heal much easier and faster this way. I am totally confident of that."

"So am I, Blair."

"So the final piece was the Bouvier School District. Could the school district be saved from financial ruin if you chose to stay? And again the answer was; 'no!' The only way we could get the money moved safely away from Rocko and Bre and get the assistance of the U.S. Attorney was to have you gone. That goes back to the admissibility of the wiretaps. This way we save the school and your family's good name."

Blair sat down beside Gordy, hugged him, and whispered, "You made the right choice, Gordy. You really did."

Gordy hugged Blair and gave her a kiss on the cheek. "Thank you, thank you so much, and please let Mac and his guys know how much I appreciate everything they've done."

Blair and Gordy had dinner on the boat before heading back to Blair's estate. Gordy marveled at the beauty of the moonlit water and the nightline of homes and condos along the gulf as they made their way back to Seaside. It had been a marvelous day in so many ways. Blair couldn't remember a more enjoyable day in years.

The next morning Gordy got up early and went jogging around Blair's estate. He loved the sights and sounds of the ocean and seagulls as he did a slow jog, which was his first in months. After breakfast Gordy headed down to the beach to try his luck fishing while Blair went to her office complex, which was adjacent to her home.

As the late afternoon sun became a little much for Gordy, he started to head back to Blair's home when he heard her call his name. Blair sat down with Gordy on her deck and said she had a couple of things she needed to go over with him.

"Gordy, I received a phone call from Reverend Durwood Hardy. He has asked that Chad McMasters and I give the eulogies at your service on Sunday. You can't tell Durwood Hardy no, so I will be flying to Bouvier for your funeral."

Gordy smiled, "That sounds really bizarre doesn't it?"

"Well, if you want bizarre, here we go. I've also been informed that Bre murdered Rocko and his teenage tramp, Jade Zeran, while they were caught having sex in her bedroom. The house has been roped off and is now a crime scene."

Gordy had a grin on his face that he was trying to suppress. "So is Bre in the Barry County Jail?"

"Not yet. The Sheriff and prosecutor are playing it smart. They have her under 24 hour surveillance until they get the ballistics report back, but you'll love the next part."

"What's that?"

"Mac's team caught the whole thing on their digital surveillance. They still had their wires in Bre's house."

"Can the taping be used by Ernie Lambert?"

"Yes! It ties perfectly in with Mac's plan to get all of the electronic surveillance into the prosecutor's hands once you were gone. Instead of just an embezzlement case, Ernie Lambert also has a murder case thanks to Bre Pattone."

"Oh my God! I can't believe it. They are paying a price finally for all the horrible things they've done."

"Yes they are, Gordy. My plan is to fly up to Bouvier on Friday evening. The house will be stocked with all the food and beer you could possibly need while I'm gone. Until we get everything settled, please stay on my grounds here until I'm back from Bouvier on Sunday evening."

"I assume you are taking your personal jet up to Bouvier?"

"Yes, my pilot, Ross, will fly us out of the Fort Walton airport. It's an easy flight to Bouvier from here."

"I will be fine. Tell everyone hi while you are there."

"Blair smiled and shook her finger, "Gordy!"

"You will talk to Emerald, won't you?

"Yes I will let her know what we've discussed. I'm looking forward to meeting Emerald."

Blair reminded Gordy to call Mac Z. LeGarge if he were to see anything suspicious. She highly doubted anything bad would happen while she was gone, but Blair didn't want to take any chances in light of everything else that transpired.

Gordy appreciated Blair's concern. He was convinced that someone would be watching close by while she was in Bouvier.

Chapter 17

Blair Jennings arrived in Bouvier on Friday evening for the first time in many years. She loved Bouvier in the fall and it certainly had a fall-like feel to it as she exited her jet at the Bouvier Municipal Airport. Standing at the airplane hanger was Durwood Hardy and his gorgeous wife, Veronica. Blair loved Reverend Hardy. She didn't know Veronica but immediately felt like she had known her for years as they talked in the back seat of the Hardy's car on their way into town.

Blair could immediately sense that the town was abuzz. It was a Friday so that meant high school football, which was the biggest social setting of the year in Bouvier. The news of Bre Pattone's arrest had made its way around town and everyone was trying to figure out everything that she was going to be charged with on Monday morning. Of course, the town was still reeling from the death of Gordy Blanchard, along with the murders of Rocko Gorski and Jade Zeran, all in the same week.

The Hardy's were taking Blair to a social gathering that had been put together by Chad McMasters, who was Gordy's best friend. The Blanchard's were having a visitation at the church on Saturday evening. Chad and several of Gordy's friends wanted to have a more relaxed setting for Gordy's closest friends to gather, swap stories, drink some beer, and remember the fun times they had experienced with Gordy. Milford and Nancy Blanchard were invited, but they graciously declined. Elizabeth Blanchard wasn't invited. Chad McMasters thoroughly disliked Elizabeth and most of his friends believed that the feeling was mutual. He had seen the hell Elizabeth had put Gordy through during their marriage and wasn't shy about occasionally telling her his thoughts.

Even though they were old enough to be everyone's parents, Raleigh J.

and Charlyn Belle Calhoun, were asked to be the hosts of the remembrance of Gordy. The Calhoun's thoroughly loved hosting events of this nature, and everyone, regardless of age, loved being around Raleigh and Charlyn Belle. When word got out that Blair Jennings would be arriving via her private jet, the invitation to the gathering became even more coveted.

Chad McMasters was thrilled to see Blair, who was stunning in her black slacks and red and black button up blouse, which accented her long blonde hair. Chad was now running the Bouvier Gazette after his father's death and his mother's decision to semi- retire from the newspaper. Chad's maturity and genuine graciousness was a pleasant surprise to Blair. Growing up in Bouvier, Chad could be a spoiled brat. It was apparent to Blair that the death of Chad's scoundrel father, Mitch McMasters, had been a calming and humanizing effect on Chad. He knew that Blair had been as close to Gordy as anyone and he was genuinely concerned about how she was holding up after hearing about the deadly explosion.

As she made her way around the room she picked up on up many of the stories that Gordy would have loved. Everyone in the room adored Gordy. They knew his faults and they also knew that he was a sincerely sweet and good person. The rare comments about Elizabeth Blanchard centered on her preoccupation with finding ways to spend the life insurance proceeds she was about to receive. One particular comment that made Blair winch was, "She's already booking condo appointments in Destin."

At one point Blair couldn't help herself. She sent a text to Gordy's new cell phone, which simply read, "Too bad you can't be here. You would really enjoy hearing all these old stories and how much everyone loves you. It sucks you can't attend your own wake."

Gordy replied back, "LOL, tell everyone I love them too......LOL. Call me later with details."

Blair was also careful to pickup on what was being said about Bre Pattone. She overhead Raleigh J. Calhoun talking to a small group. He had heard from good sources that the case against the bimbo was ironclad, solid as a Barry County rock. Rumor had it that Ernie and Buford were being assisted by the FBI in the case and Bre was going to be charged with more than just murder on Monday. No one really knew what else was coming Bre's way from a legal standpoint.

The rest of the evening consisted of various guests asking Blair for investment advice or her thoughts on when the Federal Reserve would raise short term interest rates. She enjoyed the gathering as much as she could, knowing that Gordy was alive and unlike her, these people would never get to see or talk to Gordy again.

Blair was exhausted when she arrived at Durwood and Veronica Hardy's beautiful home. They showed her to her guest room while Durwood explained that they would meet the next morning with Chad McMasters and the Blanchard's to go over the planning for the funeral service.

Before she crashed for the night, Blair called Gordy. She retold much of the night's events for him and he sounded happy that everyone was doing well and were having a good time reliving old stories. Gordy was extremely happy to hear that his parents were holding up well in light of his death. He had been worried about them and would never stop caring for their wellbeing. He was especially concerned about his mom. He knew his dad would find a way to cope, but his mom's life had centered around Milford and Gordy. He sincerely hoped his dad would help fill the void in his mom's life after the school explosion.

Blair got up early Saturday morning and he thanked Durwood and Veronica for their offer of breakfast. She begged off by telling them that she had some old friends who wanted to meet at Ruby's. They totally understood. Durwood and Blair agreed to meet at the church after her breakfast was over. She took off in one of several cars owned by the Hardy's

The breakfast crew included Chad McMasters and five others who had grown up with Gordy. Blair had asked for them to gather so she could have plenty of memories to share for the eulogy the next day, but she had another reason for the breakfast at Ruby's. She needed to meet face to face with Emerald Patrick.

Emerald greeted the breakfast crew that had organized that morning. She seated them, handed out the menus, took their drink orders, and answered questions from some of the newcomers to Ruby's. Blair was one of the few who had some questions about the menu. She did this intentionally to see how Emerald interacted with a group of strangers, not just with the Bouvier regulars. The MZL team had already provided Blair with their background synopsis on Emerald, but Blair wanted to see her in living color.

Blair immediately saw the spunky personality that Gordy had fallen in love with and also the ability to interact with others to make a business successful. Before she left the table Emerald introduced herself to all of the new faces and asked their names. When Blair introduced herself, Emerald paused and for the first time Blair saw that she was possibly nervous or flustered. Emerald recovered quickly and said, "Oh my, you're the successful hedge fund person I've heard all about. It's a pleasure to meet you."

The group had a wonderful breakfast and enjoyed their time together. Each remarked that it was a shame that it took Gordy's death to bring them together. Moments like this made Blair realize once again the unique nature of Bouvier. There were times that she missed Bouvier and moments like this were why she felt that longing.

As the breakfast was ending, Blair caught Emerald. "Emerald, you have a wonderful business. I love being able to talk to successful business people. Would you have a couple of minutes for me?"

Emerald was caught off guard by Blair's request. She smiled greatly, "You want to talk to me?"

"Yes, I'm impressed with you and what you have going on here."

"Sure, I think I'm through with my breakfast rush. How about we go the back room?"

As they sat down at one of the tables in the back room of the cafe, Blair could sense that Emerald was nervous. She wanted to calm her concerns as soon as possible. Blair started by complementing Emerald on her cafe and the atmosphere that was a result of Emerald's vibrant personality. Emerald explained her background, how she ended up finding Bouvier, and then buying Ruby's.

"It's not the prettiest story in the world, I will readily admit to that. I was a lost soul until I met Durwood Hardy. He saw something in me that no one else could see. I am forever grateful for the confidence he had in me. So that's how I came to own Ruby's Pancakes and More."

"Emerald, you are an amazing young lady. I'm very impressed, and I know someone who is also impressed and cares deeply for you, as well."

Emerald paused before she spoke, "Blair, who are you talking about?"

"I think you know who I'm referring to and I want you to know he's fine. He loves you and misses you."

Emerald began to cry. She held her head down because she didn't want anyone in the cafe to see. She whispered, "Gordy? He's ok? He misses me?"

"Yes, Emerald, he wants to be with you. Gordy loves and misses you."

"Where is he? Is he safe? Am I safe?"

"Yes he is safe and sound. Bre Pattone's actions have made things safe for you. We need to talk further before we get into Gordy's location. It would be best to talk somewhere with more privacy when we have more time."

"I'm free this afternoon. Would that work for you?"

"Great. How about 2:00 p.m.?"

"That works. Where do you want to meet?"

"When's the last time you were on an airplane?"

Emerald smiled, "I have to admit, I've never been on an airplane."

"Emerald, how about a first plane ride today? Meet me at the Bouvier Airport and we'll go for a spin in my plane."

Emerald's eyes lit up. "That's a deal! See you then."

The next part of the day was the one thing Blair was dreading - the planning meeting for Gordy's funeral. She loved Durwood Hardy and being around him made her feel good, but participating in a funeral planning meeting for someone you know is alive is pretty creepy, cold, and calculating. Blair wasn't sure how she was going to hold up when she had to see Gordy's family and friends broken and anguished over his death, which was a fraud she had helped mastermind. As she entered the Bouvier Lutheran Church, Blair reminded herself that she had to continually focus on what would have been the alternative for Gordy and his family and friends if he had stayed and faced the music. Deep down she knew that saving the Bouvier School District and Gordy's good name outweighed the anguish she would be witnessing over the next 36 hours.

Durwood, dressed casually in jeans and a white dress shirt with a Missouri State University mascot emblem on it graciously welcomed Baxter Flynn, Chad McMasters and Blair into his beautiful church office. He offered everyone some of his renowned Costa Rican coffee. All parties accepted Durwood's coffee as it was well known as the best coffee in Bouvier. Chad McMasters had been added as a funeral speaker after Durwood realized that Gordy was still alive. He wanted to lessen his role in the service and adding Chad was the smoothest way to do so. The Blanchard's thought it was a good idea as well.

Durwood began the meeting with a prayer. In it he asked for a healing hand for the Blanchard family, Gordy's friends, and the Bouvier community. He asked for guidance for each of the speakers at the service so that the light of Gordy's life could shine in this moment of remembrance. Once he concluded, Blair felt calmness come over her. It was something she hadn't felt in several weeks.

Durwood explained that the Blanchard's had been invited today but decided not to attend as they were getting ready for the visitation to be held later in the evening. He went on to let them know that the Blanchard's had met with him earlier in the week to discuss their preferences and having all three of them speaking was going to mean so much to the family. Durwood didn't convey the part that Elizabeth Blanchard had gone ballistic at the mention of Baxter Flynn being a part of the service and her quiet distain regarding the addition of Chad

McMasters.

Durwood went over the planned order of the service. To help ease his conscience, he asked Chad to read the obituary as a lead in for his remarks. Durwood had been greatly troubled by the thought of reading an obituary at the funeral service when he knew the person was still alive.

As they discussed the service, it was interesting that Durwood and Blair both knew Gordy was still living, but neither knew what the other knew. Durwood asked if everyone had their remarks prepared. Chad said he was almost done with his. Baxter stated that he had completed them a couple of days ago and was ready to talk about his best friend. Blair indicated that she wasn't ready yet, but would be ready come Sunday.

This was the first time Blair had ever met Baxter Flynn and she wasn't impressed. She keenly understood the stress he was under with the death of Gordy followed by the arrest of Bre Pattone for the embezzlement charges, but there was something about Baxter that didn't sit well with her. Part of it may have been his arrogant attitude. She sensed he was trying too hard to impress those in the room. Graciousness and warmth were definitely not part of his personality. As she sat across from Baxter, all Blair could think about was how in the world did he not know what was going on with Bre Pattone?

The meeting was classic Durwood Hardy, it lasted just long enough to cover what had to be covered and then it was over. Having had to sit through far too many meetings in his pastoral career, Durwood hated needless and endless meetings. His motto was: "Let's discuss what needs to be discussed, and then leave." Durwood also knew no one wants to sit through a long, drawn out meeting on a beautiful Saturday afternoon in September. After 17 minutes, Durwood asked everyone to join hands and they closed with a short prayer.

Once the short meeting had wrapped up, Blair and Chad talked in the church parking lot. She asked Chad for the scoop on Baxter Flynn. Chad explained that Baxter had been thrust into the Superintendent's position faster than he had expected. In turn, Gordy was placed in the assistant role much sooner than he realistically should have been. It created the perfect storm for Bre Pattone to scoop in and take advantage of the situation. Chad added, "I think he will survive in his job if everything I hear on the street is correct, but it will depend greatly on his attitude."

Blair chimed in, "I hope his A game is better than I've witnessed over the past two days. To be blunt, his attitude sucks in my opinion."

Chad liked Blair's blunt assessment, "You know Blair, I've always loved your ability to get to the heart of the matter rather quickly. I wouldn't disagree with your assessment either."

"Had Gordy said much about Baxter? Did he like working for him?"

"He never said a whole lot about Baxter. Initially, he was very appreciative of the opportunity given to him by Baxter, but after the last state audit, Gordy kind of clammed up about Baxter and his job. He wasn't his normal self in the past few weeks. I knew he was worried about the state audit that would be coming up later this month, and I assumed things were worse at home. Elizabeth had been brutal to him after the last audit. His self esteem seemed to bottom out after her daily brow beatings. She was embarrassed it would look bad for her and her social standing with her co-workers. She's vicious!"

Chad invited Blair to a late lunch, but she asked for a rain check as she had a previous commitment. He assumed Blair was seeing the Blanchard's. Little did he know that she was going to spend time with Emerald Patrick.

Emerald showed up at the Bouvier Municipal Airport right on time. She was dressed causally but still looked very attractive. Blair could definitely see why Gordy was smitten with her. Emerald walked around the plane twice and began asking lots of questions. Blair could tell that Emerald was really looking forward to their plane adventure.

Blair explained that the plane was a Cessna Citation Encore, which would get them to any part of the continental United States from Bouvier in less than two hours.

Once they entered the plane Emerald was in awe of the inside of the cabin. She loved the comfort of the light brown leather seats. As she leaned back in her cushy seat, Emerald asked, "How do you keep from going to sleep as soon as this thing takes off?"

Blair was enjoying watching Emerald take in the plane.

"Emerald, I nod off a lot while on the plane. It seems like this can be my one time period to be away from the world. It can be very relaxing in flight, and Ross is an excellent pilot."

Ross informed Blair that he was ready for take off.

As soon as Ross departed for the plane's cabin, Emerald leaned over with a mischievous grin, "Ok, I know this is very forward and probably rude, but how much does a plane like this cost?"

Blair smiled as she was clearly not offended at all by Emerald's question.

"Emerald, I honestly don't know."

"You don't know how much your plane costs? Now that must be nice."

Blair laughed hysterically, "No, no, it's not like that. I participate in an airplane leasing service. I pay an annual fee and in return I have access to this and other planes depending upon the number of passengers and the destination. The service also provides a pilot."

"Do you have different pilots?"

"You can, but I made a deal with them several years ago for Ross to be my pilot. He's very good at what he does and I don't have to worry about him going out partying during the down time of a trip and then showing up hung-over to fly me home. He may not have much of a personality, but he's a great person and excellent pilot. I try to treat Ross great on trips."

Both got silent as Ross taxied down the runway, made the ascent, and was airborne over Bouvier. Ross made one pass over Bouvier before he turned the plane to the southeast. Emerald was enjoying the takeoff and the view of the beautiful area from the sky.

Once Ross had headed in the direction she had chosen, Blair turned to Emerald, "How about an early dinner?"

"Sure, what do you have in mind?"

"I have to be back for the visitation, so it would be a quick trip. When was the last time you've been to the Destin - Panama City Beach area of Florida?"

Emerald laughed, "This girl doesn't get out of Barry County with a cafe to run seven days a week. So it would have to have been back in my party days, which would have been a long time ago. Probably back in college."

Blair enjoyed Emerald's candor. "Well, it's changed a lot since you were there, assuming you remember it since you said you were on spring break."

Emerald smiled at Blair's line. "You've got that right. I remember part of the trip, but to be honest with you, at that point of my life I wasn't making the greatest decisions. There are parts of the trip that are still a blur to me."

"I totally understand, Emerald. I was young once, as well."

Emerald leaned toward Blair, "This morning you said Gordy is safe and sound. Can we talk about his location, what he's doing, where he intends to go?"

Blair reached down to pick up a black leather pouch and from it she pulled out some papers which had the appearance of a contract. In fact, it was a confidentiality agreement. Blair handed the document to Emerald, "Please look this over, Emerald, and let me know what you think. If it meets with your approval, then we will discuss the questions you have."

Emerald began to read the document. As she got to the heart of the agreement, she began to cry. As tears started to flow onto the document, Blair knew instantly that Emerald was caught off guard by her gesture and her tears were tears of joy, not sorrow. Emerald stopped reading and looked over at Blair, "I can't believe this! You can't be serious, can you? You would do this for me; I should say Gordy and me?"

"Yes, Emerald, I would and I will. So you are agreeable to the terms of this agreement?"

"Heavens yes I am. Who would turn down something as wonderful as this? I can't believe this! When Gordy would come in for breakfast we would get to talking about stuff. One day we were talking about our favorite places to visit. Gordy was talking about how much he loved the gulf coast. I mentioned that it would be a dream to have my own cafe business in a quiet beach community. That little stinker remembered the conversation. I am floored." At this point Emerald began to cry again.

"Gordy definitely remembered the conversation. Would you like to see the place I have in mind?"

"Oh my, yes!"

"Great, we will be there in less that 45 minutes by the way Ross is hauling this thing today, but before we land, please read the document fully. If you are in total agreement you can sign the document. If you have any doubts at all, you are welcome to have a reputable attorney review it for you and answer any questions you might have."

It didn't' take long for Emerald to finish reading the confidentiality agreement which provided her with a graduated ownership interest in a beachfront cafe located near Seaside, Florida. The ownership interest would revert back to a corporation owned by Blair if Emerald ever violated the confidentiality terms of the agreement, which essentially meant she would never reveal the existence of Milford T. Blanchard, Jr. - or his new existence as Gordon Blansford.

Emerald signed the document on the spot. She was beaming, "So what's the scoop on the cafe?"

"It's a neat place, right on the beach, and is very popular. However, the owners are getting older and the place needs a shot in the arm. The owners realize that and that's why they want to sell. It's a seven day a week job during the season. They close down around the first of November each year and reopen around the first of March. The books on the place are very good. If you run it like Ruby's you will make a lot of money."

"Should we keep the same name or go with something new?"

"Great question. I would recommend changing the name. It's a popular place; however the owners have gotten cranky in the past couple of years. A new name would signal to the public that it's in new hands. I like the name: Emerald's."

Emerald began to cry again. "I love it.!!! I will ask again, why would you do this? It is so incredibly wonderful. You are incredibly wonderful."

Blair smiled, she reached over and held Emerald's hand, "That's very sweet. You have no idea how good it feels to hear those kind words. Like

I said, the why is something we will talk about on one of those lazy days on the beach when we all have a day off to do absolutely nothing."

"I can't wait. But I do have a concern with me having a business in Seaside, and Gordy living in Seaside, won't that compromise the ability to hide him?"

"Gordy won't be in the business. He can't be. There are way too many people from Bouvier that come down here to vacation to have him assisting you inside the restaurant. Plus, word will get out in Bouvier that you now own a cafe here. Gordy wants to do something else. Plus, in a month or so he will not look exactly like himself."

"He's having plastic surgery?"

"The world's foremost plastic surgeon is one of my clients. He will be performing the operation."

"I know he has to change some. But you're not going to drastically change the looks of the Gordy that I love, are you?"

Blair smiled, "No need to worry, Emerald. Gordy will look as good as ever. The procedure will not radically change him. It will consist of a few minor changes to allow plausible deniability if he were to ever run into someone from Bouvier. This way he would get the 'You look kind of like Gordy Blanchard,' instead of 'You are Gordy Blanchard.' And Gordy has seen the planned diagram of what the surgeon plans to achieve and he is totally fine with it."

"This may be a stupid question, but I'm not going to have to change my identity or undergo identity changing plastic surgery as a part of the deal?"

Blair loved the question and was laughing so hard she could hardly talk. "No, no, Emerald, you can continue to be Emerald Patrick as long as you so choose."

Prior to landing, Ross circled the beach to give Blair and Emerald a sky view of the beach cafe. Emerald was ecstatic when she saw the cafe and was even more excited when she and Blair walked into the establishment. The prime vacation season may have ended but the joint was still hopping late Saturday afternoon. The music was flowing through the cafe and it was a lively scene. In addition to several tourists, a group of locals were hanging at the bar area watching college football with the beach and ocean in the background.

Emerald had a chance to meet the owners. They were a nice couple and Emerald could clearly see that they were ready to retire. Blair explained that the closing of the purchase would take place after November 1, allowing Emerald the entire winter to get everything in order in both Bouvier and Seaside.

The only down point in the trip was when Emerald asked if Gordy would be joining them for lunch. Blair explained that it was simply too risky for the three of them to be in public at this time. Emerald understood, but Blair could see that she was really wanting to see Gordy.

After a great lunch of fish tacos, ice tea, and frozen margaritas, they returned to Bouvier just in time for Gordy's visitation. Blair had thoroughly enjoyed spending the afternoon with Emerald. She knew that Gordy had seen something special in her and she had now witnessed the same thing. Blair was almost as excited about spending the upcoming months helping Gordy and Emerald start their new life together as Emerald was. Emerald could hardly contain her excitement at the prospect of her new life with Gordy in Seaside, Florida, but she understood the utmost importance of acting normal in the days ahead. Blair had continually drilled home that fact during the flight back to Bouvier.

After they departed the jet, Blair and Emerald hugged. Blair made her way to a visitation that she was dreading and Emerald went back to Ruby's to check on the evening dinner attendance. In her mind, Emerald was already counting down the days until she opened Emerald's on the beach.

Chapter 18

The sun rose on Sunday morning in Bouvier for what would be a radiant September day in the Ozarks. Blair got up earlier than she normally would because of her desire to have breakfast with the Hardy's and their daughter, Caroline, who was a childhood friend of hers. As she made her way to the Hardy's beautiful kitchen, Blair found Durwood in his study. When she walked in, Durwood was in deep thought as he was listening to a beautiful classical music piece, Bach's Concerto No. 7 in G minor.

Durwood looked up from his trance to see Blair walk into his elaborate study, which was filled with everything from great works of literature to modern fiction. He was a great lover of John Grisham's books. She could tell that he was happy to see her and she could also discern that Durwood was not as ease this morning. She assumed he was getting his mind around all that he had to cover that day, which included preaching his normal Sunday morning service at the Bouvier Lutheran Church and then the memorial service for Gordy in the afternoon.

Blair loved the sound coming from Durwood's study, "That is beautiful, Durwood. Is that Bach?"

"Yes, it's Bach's Concerto number 7 in G minor. I was right; I thought you were a fan of Bach's. When I'm tense or stressed I put it on and it really helps calm the ole nerves. That along with a great cup of coffee." They both laughed, which seemed to help Durwood's nerves.

"I do the same when I'm stressed. It's amazing how relaxing music can be. Durwood, it's a busy day ahead for you."

"Yes it is. I guess this is a sign of my age. I'm actually more stressed today than I have been in quite some time. This is a tough service. So many have been impacted by Gordy. It's not that Gordy was a great leader

- which we know he isn't, I mean he wasn't, but he was our guy. He was so likable, genuine, kind, funny, just someone you liked to be around. That's what has resonated with the community."

"The outpouring of support at last night's visitation was unbelievable."

"It really was. Gordy's reputation, his young age, combined with the Blanchard's reputation has resulted in the tremendous expression of compassion from the community. You always have a large group at a visitation when someone dies young, but this was an amazing tribute. I think the family was very appreciative of the support from the community. Elizabeth and Nancy seemed to be amazed by the crowd. I'm sure Milford was less so. He seemed to have the mindset of 'if this isn't the biggest visitation ever, I'm going to be offended.' That's terrible of me to say, but it's the truth."

Blair nodded in approval. "I talked to the family last night. They were very gracious, especially Nancy. I've always loved her. I tried to be around Elizabeth as little as possible. She drives me up the wall after being around her for more than three minutes. Milford still seemed to be in a daze."

"I try to stay away from him as much as possible as well and I think the feeling is mutual. Oh, before I forget, I spoke with Emerald last night to see how she was holding up and she was on cloud nine after her jet excursion. It was her first ever airplane flight. Thanks for reaching out to her."

Blair was caught off guard when Durwood brought up Emerald. She tried to act normal, but she immediately wondered how much Emerald had told her pastor about the afternoon plane ride.

"You're welcome, Durwood. She is a very sweet young lady. I enjoyed the heck out of our afternoon together."

"It was incredibly sweet of you to reach out to her. I guess you know that she and Gordy had become close prior to the explosion."

Again, Blair wondered if Durwood was fishing for information or simply being sweet as he always was.

"Yes, I was aware they were talking quite a bit from my conversations with Gordy before the event. You don't have to worry; there wasn't an affair with Emerald."

"I know, but I hate to say it, but it was headed in that direction. In my position, unfortunately I've witnessed and counseled a lot of couples in divorce situations, and most affairs start innocently. Things aren't the best at home and all of the sudden there is someone who is the friend, who fills an emotional void of some nature. The next thing you know, things are out of control. It's very similar to when someone starts stealing. It usually starts small and then it builds to a point where they can no longer conceal their actions."

Blair was starting to sweat it. She was wondering if Durwood knew way more than she could possibly imagine. First he brings up Emerald and then he ventures into stealing. Her plan was to move the conversation along without appearing to be frazzled.

"Has Elizabeth been saying anything about Gordy and Emerald?"

"I haven't heard anything since last Sunday. Since then I have been told that she is focused on the life insurance money that is coming her way. But prior to last Sunday, I was told that she was incensed by the increased time Gordy and Emerald were spending together at Ruby's. The attention in the community has shifted to Bre Pattone. I guess that tomorrow she will be charged with murder for the deaths at her home and possibly Gordy's. And the other story is she embezzled money from the school. You hear anything from a small figure to millions. Apparently,

Ernie Lambert wanted to wait until after Gordy's service to formally charge Bre."

Blair continued to wonder how much Durwood really knew about Gordy, Emerald, and the embezzlement. She also picked up on the point that Durwood never talked about Gordy's death. He kept referring to the 'event' or 'last Sunday,' but she had noticed that he had not said anything about Gordy's death.

"How much truth do you think there is to the various stories?"

"I sincerely hope and pray that the story about Bre embezzling millions isn't true. That could bankrupt the school. It could be catastrophic, but I've learned not to get worked up over these things. I'm confident that we have smart people who could keep things of this horrible nature from happening. But enough about what I think, what are you thoughts on this Blair? You're the one who manages billions of dollars every day."

Blair nervously smiled. She was wondering is she was being played by the legendary Durwood Hardy, but she decided to continue to play along if that was Durwood's intent.

"You know, Durwood, you are right. I've also learned not to worry about things beyond my control. And you're also right; usually someone smart will step up and prevent something catastrophic from happening. So, if you are asking for my two cents, I suspect that the school will be fine, once all the dust settles."

Durwood liked what he heard. He gracefully stood and asked Blair to join him for breakfast. As they made their way to the Hardy's kitchen Durwood uttered, "I just pray nothing else comes up. We just can't take much more as a community."

Before Blair could ask Durwood what he meant by this comment they were soon joined by Durwood's gorgeous wife, Veronica, and his daughter, Caroline Hardy. Caroline had stopped in Springfield earlier that morning for some delicious bagels and muffins.

After an enjoyable breakfast, which gave Blair and Caroline an opportunity to catch up with what was going on in each other's lives; Blair attended the 10:45 a.m. at the Bouvier Lutheran Church. It had been too long since she had heard Durwood Hardy speak from the church pulpit. She had always known that he was a talented speaker, but she had forgotten just how incredibly captivating Durwood was in the pulpit. In her professional life Blair had been provided the opportunity to hear many motivational speakers - including U.S. Presidents. She had to admit to herself that Durwood Hardy was either the best or one of the top three she had ever witnessed in person. Durwood's moving message helped get everyone's minds temporarily off the looming funeral service that afternoon.

A capacity crowd of more than 1,750 filled the Bouvier Lutheran Church for the memorial service to celebrate the life of Milford T. Blanchard, Jr. otherwise known as Gordy. Durwood had never seen a crowd this large for a funeral service in Bouvier. It was even larger than the gathering for his first wife's funeral, which most Bouvier residents had remarked at the time that it was the largest funeral they had ever attended. The introit music was played by Marlene Beckworth, the legendary pianist for the church. She proudly and gracefully touched the ivories of the black grand piano as the Blanchard family walked down the center isle and took their seats at the front of the beautiful sanctuary. Blair began to cry when she saw Gordy's mother walking and weeping into the church. At that moment, she wished she could tell her the truth about Gordy and make everything right with her.

The Bouvier High School All Girls Choir began the service with a beautiful performance of "Amazing Grace." After welcoming the crowd for coming to pay their respects, Durwood introduced Chad McMasters, who was able to read the obituary without breaking down, in spite of his concerns prior to the service. Chad followed with stories of good times he and Gordy had shared together. He alternated between having the crowd laughing and crying. Chad concluded by saying he would always feel like he had Gordy looking down to help guide him in his journey. "And if the Cards make it to the World Series this year, I'm buying two seats and will have Gordy's old Cardinals jersey sitting right beside me, as if he were with me all the way to another Cardinals championship." When Chad walked away from the podium there wasn't a dry eye in the sanctuary.

Blair spoke next for six minutes. She broke the ice by playfully chiding Chad for being such a tough act to follow. Her theme was Gordy as a loyal friend who could be trusted and counted upon regardless of the situation. Blair shared a fun moment about the time that she, Gordy, and Chad broke out of the Bouvier Lutheran Church nursery when they were four years old, leaving the nursery attendant in a state of hysteria. Just as they were about to make their way to the church play ground, they saw Milford T. Blanchard looking out the back window of the church. Not sure how to handle being caught, Blair recalled Gordy saying, "Wave great big. Dad won't be as mad if we can make him laugh." Blair said this symbolized Gordy's outlook on life, where he was very successful at making others feel at ease regardless of the gravity of the situation.

"I thought it was fitting that the firefighters were able to find his Bouvier class ring. He loved Bouvier and he loved all of you so very much. I know because since I live far away, I would call Gordy to catch up on what was going on in Bouvier. He would always tell me about what was going well and who he was worried about. He cared deeply about his family, his school, and the town of Bouvier more than any of you will ever know." That was a coded message to explain why Gordy did what he did. It was his only way to save Bouvier.

Baxter Flynn came to the podium and looked as if he might throw up at any moment. His planned remarks were supposed to last approximately four to five minutes. However, due to his nervousness he began to ramble. He began to share stories which were primarily about himself with very little relevance on the life of Gordy Blanchard. After nine excruciating minutes Baxter Flynn walked away front the podium to the relief of nearly everyone in the church.

After much prayer and deliberation, Durwood Hardy spoke on the life lessons he had gained from knowing Gordy and from the shocking explosion seven days earlier.

"I'm not here to say good bye to my friend, Gordy, because I am confident that I will see him again. I know he's not far away and he cares deeply about everyone here." Blair winced when she heard Durwood's words. "The last time I spoke with Gordy, he was worried about many things, just like anyone with a lot on their plate. It was a testament to how much he cared about his community. We talked and prayed and then he gave me that smile that was infectious, and I reminded him what we had always talked about. He smiled again, 'Focus on what you can control and have a plan.' Gordy had a plan, and because of that plan, I am confident that I will see Gordy in the near future." Once again, Blair was caught off guard by Durwood's comments, but she definitely didn't plan to broach the topic with Durwood at any time.

Durwood concluded by emphasizing the importance of unintended consequences. "We are all better off because of Gordy. It may have been a simple hello that brightened our day or a decision in his job at the school, but I am totally confident that Gordy made a positive impact on each and every one of us here today. I ask that we continue to remember his impact and how each of us have the power of positive unintended consequences in what we do, say, and how we act in our daily lives. We can all make a difference."

After a short prayer by Durwood, the service concluded at the fifty-five minute mark with a moving rendition of "It Is Well with My Soul" by the Bouvier High School boy's quartet.

The nearly empty casket carrying what was believed to be the skeletal remains of Gordy Blanchard was laid to rest in the Bouvier Community Cemetery, which overlooked the beautiful town. In the days leading up to the explosion, Gordy had found an extra skeleton set in the attic of the high school biology lab. He had placed the skeleton in his desk prior to the explosion and had placed his Bouvier Class ring on the right index finger of the skeleton. Gordy figured it would be years before anyone would discover that the extra skeleton was missing from the biology lab attic.

After a much needed nap, Blair and the Hardy's were the guests of Raleigh J. and Charlyn Belle Calhoun for a wonderful Sunday evening dinner. After what had been a stressful and eventful day, a lively and pleasurable dinner at the Calhoun's was just what Blair and the Hardy's needed. Once dinner was over, Raleigh congratulated Blair and Durwood for their thoughtful and meaningful words at the memorial service. Raleigh then began to discuss what he was hearing 'on the street,' regarding the case against Bre Pattone.

"From what I'm hearing, before he died, it sounds like Gordy saved the school and possibly the town of Bouvier from total financial chaos."

Durwood leaned forward, "How did this happen, Raleigh?"

"Well, from what I've been told, in addition to murder, Bre is going to be charged with multi-million dollar embezzlement for funds taken from the Bouvier School District. She and that greasy haired goon boyfriend were going to kill Gordy and take off with the money. Somehow Gordy got wind of what Bre was doing, notified the authorities, and the money was intercepted before Bre and that goon could take off with it. It's a shame Gordy isn't alive to see what he did to save the school."

Blair noticed that Durwood sat in silence and let the wives go on and on about the tragic death of Gordy Blanchard. She didn't know who was spinning the story, but she was greatly impressed by the way in which they were making Gordy out to be a hero. Blair assumed Milford T. Blanchard was playing a part in drafting the Gordy as a hero storyline. The enjoyable evening with the Calhoun's wrapped up early as all had busy Monday morning schedules.

Around the same time that the dinner with the Calhoun's had wrapped up, Gordy Blanchard was sitting on the deck of Blair's home as he had done most of the day. The pain and guilt resulting from his actions were starting to get to him, combined with the feeling of isolation. He couldn't get out of his mind the torment that his parents were going through on what was the worst day of their lives. Gordy began to feel nauseous. He also began to have suicidal thoughts. At that moment, the isolation was drowning out all of the reasons why he did what he did. He couldn't see a single positive thing from his life and Gordy was seriously wondering if he could make it through the night.

As he began to pace the meandering deck overlooking the gulf, his new cell vibrated. It was a text message. One that he assumed was from Blair, but it was from another phone number - one that looked very familiar. As he slid the message icon, Gordy's eyes saw the following message: "You did the right thing. You saved the school and town."

Gordy was shaking as he read and re-read the message and the phone number. Suddenly he recalled the phone number, it was Durwood Hardy's.

Crying uncontrollably, Gordy replied back: "Thank you so much. You have no idea how much those words mean to me."

Chapter 19

Blair got up and around early Monday morning. She begged off breakfast with the Hardy's as she explained that she needed to go to the Barry County Justice Center to sign paperwork to open up the Estate of Milford T. Blanchard, Jr., for which she would be the Executor. What she didn't disclose was she would also be going to meet with Ernie Lambert to sign the document releasing to the Bouvier School District the funds stolen by Bre Patttone, which Blair's financial firm had been able to intercept before they left the United States.

Blair Jennings arrived at Ernie Lambert's office precisely at 8:00 a.m. Per the court order prepared by the FBI and U.S. Attorney's office in Tallahassee, Blair signed the authorization for her financial firm to wire transfer to the Bouvier School District $6,475,000. Before signing the authorization, she emphasized to Ernie that it was in everyone's best interests for him to reach a quick plea deal with Bre Pattone on the murder charges. She related in no uncertain terms that a trial for Bre on the embezzlement charges would not be pretty for anyone involved in the case.

"Ernie, my name should never come up in the prosecution of Bre Pattone. So many laws were broken in order to save the Bouvier School District I can't even begin to count. Get your plea deal, send her ass to prison for life, and call it a day."

Ernie assured Blair that he would follow her wishes. He thanked her profusely for her assistance and asked Blair if she wanted to meet with Baxter Flynn to inform him of the return of the embezzled funds. Blair politely declined. She had seen enough of Baxter Flynn over the past three days and had no desire to see him again.

Before she left his office, Ernie asked Blair, "Are you confident that you found everything?

"Yes, why?

"And you are confident that Bre didn't have any other help? Specifically, no signs of Baxter Flynn being involved?"

Blair smiled after hearing Ernie's question, "No, but I don't have a good feeling about the little bastard."

Ernie laughed, "Neither do I."

An hour later in the rotunda of the Barry County Justice Center, in the presence of reporters and TV cameras, Ernie Lambert announced the arrest of Bre Pattone for the murder of Rocko Gorski and Jade Zeran, conspiracy to murder Milford T. Blanchard, Jr., and the embezzlement of $6,475,000 from the Bouvier School District. He then stood with Baxter Flynn and handed him a replica check of $6,475,000 from the FBI representing the recapture of the stolen money from the school district. Before he concluded the press conference, Ernie made the following statement, "There is one person I wish I could thank at this time and that's Gordy Blanchard. Before he died, Gordy alerted authorities that something was wrong at the Bouvier School District. That call my have cost him his life, but it saved the Bouvier School District and to be honest, the town of Bouvier."

As Blair watched the press conference, she marveled at the spin being put on the facts. She was quite confident that it was the work of Raleigh J. Calhoun and Durwood Hardy. Blair also knew that Gordy's parents would be very proud of their son after seeing the press conference. The other thing that went through her mind was whether the photo op with Ernie Lambert would cost or save Baxter Flynn's job at the Bouvier School District.

Once the press conference concluded, Blair knew that her work was concluded as well. She called Ross and asked him to have the jet ready to fly back to Seaside. Her mission was accomplished.

After Buford Blakeley's crew wrapped up the inventory of Bre Patttone and Jade Zeran's home they discovered that Rocko Gorski was planning a double cross of Bre Pattone. Buford's crew discovered one way plane tickets to San Paulo, Brazil for Rocko and Jade. They were going to leave Bre high and dry. The flight had been delayed because Rocko had lost his driver's license a few days prior to the intended get out of the country flight. Unbeknownst to Buford and his crew was the fact that Rocko's driver's license had been lifted by Mac Z. LeGarge's team. In order to set up a fictitious investment account for Rocko Gorski to facilitate the recovery of the stolen funds for school, Blair Jennings had to have a copy of Rocko's driver's license. If the MZL team hadn't been able to pull that off, the plan to recover the funds and thus save the school could have unraveled.

After reviewing the cell phone records of Rocko Gorski, investigators discovered that on the day of his death, Gorski had repeatedly called a bank in Hattiesburg, Mississippi. This was the bank that Rocko had used to park the embezzled school funds before his plan to leave the country for good as a rich man.

Blakeley's investigators also discovered that on the day of his death, Rocko was desperate to find out what had happened to the funds in his account. The bank informed him that all of the funds had been wired out to an investment company earlier that day, per his signed authorization. Rocko had become belligerent. All day long he continued to call virtually every member of the bank's management team demanding his money and threatening all sorts of lawsuits. Then late that afternoon, the phone calls from Mr. Gorski stopped. The bank was surprised when they stopped hearing from the irate Mr. Gorski the next day.

Little did they know that they would never hear from Rocko Gorski ever again until they received a phone call from the Sheriff of Barry County, Missouri. Buford Blakeley took great pride in telling Barkley Primrose, the President of the Valley Crest Bank and Trust in Hattiesburg, "You won't be hearing from that thug anymore."

"Why do you say that, Mr. Blakeley?"

"Because he's dead. Dead as a door nail."

"Oh, I'm sorry to hear. Please express our condolences to his family."

Buford laughed, "Save your breath, I'm sure they are glad the greasy bastard is gone as well."

A rattled Primrose concluded, "Oh, well it's indeed been a pleasure to speak with you today, Mr. Blakeley."

Buford Blakeley laughed heartily at the thought of the entire bank in Hattiesburg, Mississippi being worried sick about the prospect of being sued for more than six million dollars by a thug like Rocko Gorski. He was also smiling at the prospect of getting to go check in on his latest inmate at the Barry County Jail, Ms. Bre Pattone.

Late on Monday morning, Emerald Patrick dropped by Durwood Hardy's office. She wanted to let him know that she was going to be out of town for a couple of weeks to take a much needed vacation. She didn't offer her destination and Durwood didn't ask. However, he knew it would more than likely be Seaside, Florida and she wouldn't be vacationing alone. Durwood was quite confident that if he ever wanted to see Gordy Blanchard, or whatever his new name was, he would probably run into him in Seaside - probably at a golf course.

Emerald gave Durwood a long hug and told him that she would be in touch. He could tell that she had tears in her eyes when she left his office. As she departed, Durwood said a silent prayer for Emerald, Gordy, Blair, and what he presumed to be their new life together.

The next few weeks of Ernie Lambert's life were filled with the various frivolous motions being filed by Rex Moffitt on behalf of his notorious client, Bre Pattone. The first was a motion to reduce the bail set at 10 million dollars by Judge Claibourn. Next, was a motion to exhume the bodies of Rocko Gorski and Jade Zeran in order to have another independent autopsy performed. Next, was a civil rights violation motion. All of the filings by Rex Moffitt were summarily denied by Judge Claibourn.

Rex Moffitt had made it abundantly clear that he would use the battered woman defense for Bre. They were placing all the blame for the embezzlement at the hands of Rocko Gorski. Their line was that Rocko had beaten Bre into submission. She ultimately reached he point that she couldn't take it any longer and began stealing funds to save her life.

Ernie Lambert was becoming worried that the battered woman defense might possibly work for Bre, until she was caught having sex with a jailer and then attempted to flee the jail after the late night romp.

Blair Jennings kept close track of everything going on with the Bre Pattone case. One thing was clear, no way were Rex or Bre going to try to place any blame on Gordy Blanchard. Going after Gordy was a sure fire ticket to death row for Bre.

Upon hearing the latest Bre news, Blair was confident that Ernie Lambert would have no problem obtaining a plea deal, thus averting an embarrassing trial.

Chapter 20

The winter was a busy time for Emerald and Gordy. She completed all of her desired renovations to Emerald's on the Beach. Gordy had successful reconstructive surgery. The recovery was more painful that he had anticipated, but the end result was exactly what he, Blair, and Emerald had envisioned. Blair was easing Gordy into his desired field of sports psychology. His first venture was working with members of the Florida State golf team. He loved what he was doing as he seemed to have an instant rapport with the team and it appeared that his methods were helping several members of the team as they headed into the conference portion of their golf schedule.

Gordy Blanchard had become much more loved and popular in his death than he ever could have been alive. The narrative that he had saved the school and the community just before his death had become so strong that the Bouvier Board of Education was considering a proposal to rename the Bouvier High School Gymnasium to the Gordy Blanchard Memorial Court.

Seven months later, while taking his annual spring golf vacation in Destin, Florida, Chad McMasters received a call from Emerald Patrick. Since he was in the area, Emerald wanted Chad to come by and be one of the first customers in her new establishment on the beach in Seaside, Florida simply named Emerald's.

"Lunch tomorrow is on me, Chad."

"Sounds, great, Emerald. I can't wait to see you and your new digs. See you at one o'clock tomorrow."

The next day, Chad McMasters arrived right at one o'clock and was

Author's Note

In writing The Flight of the Slacker I was provided with invaluable assistance by my wonderful wife, Darla, and my dear friend, Kerry Hays. A sincere thank you goes to each of them for their gracious advice and support. I couldn't have written this book without their guidance.

I also want to note that I serve on a local school board. It is my pleasure to serve a great school district. The school is led by an incredibly talented, honest and dedicated team. Rest assured, Gordy Blanchard, Baxter Flynn, and Bre Pattone don't exist at the school that I proudly serve.

The front cover photo was produced by Jeremy Huse of Jeremy Huse Photography. Thanks to Jeremy for his work to get the photo just right. Additionally, thanks to Jake Whitham for his assistance with the cover pic.

seated on the upstairs deck of Emerald's, which provided one of the most gorgeous views of the gulf waters of any area restaurant. Chad was taking in the incredible view on a beautiful sunny April day when a very pregnant Emerald Patrick appeared at his table.

As he stood up to give Emerald a hug, Chad burst out, "Wow, it has been a productive winter for you, Emerald! Who's the lucky guy?"

Before Emerald could answer, a familiar voice came from behind Chad, "Well, are the Cards going to win it all this year?"

Chad immediately recognized the voice, with the slow Ozark's accent. He quickly turned around to see someone who greatly resembled Gordy Blanchard. Chad stood motionless for several moments before he could even talk, "Oh my God, this really can't be happening!"

Gordy hugged Chad and whispered, "It really is, buddy, it really is."

Jon Horner

The Flight of the Slacker is the latest work by Jon Horner. Horner's previously published novels, The Rev of Bouvier and The Deadly News, have become popular with fan's of his novels which center around the scandalous fictional town of Bouvier, Missouri.

Jon Horner is a novelist, motivational speaker, community leader, and successful community bank president. He lives in Cassville, Missouri, with his wife Darla and their children, Chase and Madison.

To inquire about Jon's motivational and leadership speaking opportunities, please contact him at www.jonhorner.net